pieces

of

16

An anthology of creative writing

Eagle River Secondary
Sicamous, BC
2016

ISBN 978-1532945922

© Eagle River Secondary 2016

Eagle Screech Publishing

The authors maintain all copyright to their individual work.

Pieces of 16: An anthology of creative writing

Edited by Shawn Bird

Eagle River Secondary

PO Box 9

Sicamous, BC

V0E 2V0

www.ers.sd83.bc.ca

ers@sd83.bc.ca

pieces

of

16

An anthology of creative writing

Eagle River Secondary

Sicamous, BC

2016

    This anthology represents the work of students in a variety of writing courses at the small but mighty Eagle River Secondary in Sicamous, BC. With only 125 students in grade 8 to 12, ERS offers programs reflecting a variety of cross-grade, cross-curricular innovations. Our morning 'core' program involves six week project-problem-inquiry based learning cross-curricular competency assessed courses for grades 8-10. In the afternoon we have cross-grade trimester electives, like the grade 8-12 Creative Writing class. Under the guidance of librarian, counselor, career coordinator, and English teacher Shawn Bird, the students explore ways to tell story or express their experiences.

    The selections in this anthology were written by students from age 13 to 19. Some students have chosen to write under a pseudonym. The Creative Writing class worked on huge projects this year, aiming for 10,000 to 25,000 words during the course. Enjoy excerpts from these large projects. Not all students chose to submit work for this anthology.

Please note: some pieces have language and content warnings.

Table of

Core class: Short Story

Bethany	Shattered Glass	**31**
Cydney	The Cat Life	**24**
Elene	I Trusted You	**10**
Emily	Me, Myself and I	**19**
Jade	Played	**34**
León	All Else Fails	**16**
Nicole	Not Everyone Values Your Trust	**37**
Tiffany	Friendship Is Nothing Without Trust	**28**
Tristyn	Trust Can Be Lost in Seconds	**21**
Veronica	Pirate's Trust	**13**

Core class: Poetry

Fallon	I Miss	**262**
	The Smallest Things	**263**
Jordann	Warnings	**258**
	Isn't It Funny?	**259**
Liz	We Are Women	**267**
Natasha	She Knows	**260**
	Breath	**261**
Niah	Innocence	**264**
Tiffany	Books	**265**
	Black out poem	**266**

Contents

Creative Writing class

Andrew	The Arise (excerpt)	**190**
Armando	Free (excerpt)	**197**
	Your Time is Up (poem)	**252**
	Grilled life (poem)	**253**
Autumn	Eyland (excerpt)	**42**
Brandon	Skate Dreams (excerpt)	**114**
Celeste	Six Months (excerpt of verse novella)	**210**
	Leave (poem)	**246**
Garrett	The Depth (excerpt)	**149**
Hannah	A Christmas Murder (excerpt)	**174**
	Devil (poem)	**247**
Hayley	The Memory Forager (excerpt of verse novel)	**68**
	Ice Cream (poem)	**242**
Jessie	Secrets of a Songbird (excerpt)	**101**
	Songbird (poem)	**249**
	To Be Enough (poem)	**251**
Kevin	As I Fly (poem)	**245**
León	Samurai Beat (excerpt)	**48**
Liz	An Unexpected Turn (excerpt)	**236**
	The Same Shoes (poem)	**254**
Veronica	Wild Groves (excerpt)	**131**
	Embrace (poem)	**244**
Will	Everything All Healing (poem)	**248**

Core: Short Story Class

Short, short stories

on a theme of lost trust

Elene:

I Trusted You

Marcella stormed out of the school right as the bell rang. *How dare she tell them that!* She thought angrily.

Amy hurried after her "Marcella wait! I didn't mean to!"

Marcella didn't slow down to let her old friend catch up.

"Marcella stop!" Amy shouted, still trying to catch up.

Marcella sighed finally slowing down. "What do you want?" She said, glaring at Amy. Her long brown hair which was pulled back in a ponytail swished behind her like an angry cat's tail.

"I'm sorry! I didn't mean to tell them! They made me do it!" Amy said.

Marcella rolled her eyes. "This is the third time you've done this."

Amy looked away. "Come on, you know I didn't do it on purpose!"

Every single time you've done this it was on purpose. Marcella thought, glaring at Amy angrily. They both fell silent as other people from their school walk by, giving them curious looks.

"Marcella, please trust me..." Amy whispered looking at her again.

Marcella shook her head "Why should I? All you've done is tell three of the most judgmental people I know things you promised not to tell anyone! Everyone in the school knows now!" She felt tears stinging. *No! I won't cry in front of her!* She blinked a few times, holding them back. "Marcella I won't do it ag-"

"You said that last time and look where we are now!"

Amy's eyes widened.

They fell silent again, the only noise coming from the wind in the trees. "Why? Why did you do it?" Marcella said softly

Amy sighed..."Marcel- Are you crying?"

Marcella quickly rubbed her eyes, shaking her head. She looked at the sleeves on her hoodie and saw the smears of her eye makeup.

Amy looked at her shocked. "I-I'm sorry" Amy stammered.

"Oh, you're sorry? Sorry doesn't fix anything when you keep doing it over and over." The tears were streaming down Marcella's face now. *I won't tell you any more secrets,* Marcella thought. Amy stared at her like she wanted to say something, but she kept quiet then Amy turned away. Then she stopped and looked at her again. "I thought if I told them... they wouldn't judge me too..." Amy hung her head, "I'm so sorry."

Marcella turned away and started walking home. She softly whispered, "I trusted you Amy..."

Marcella could feel Amy staring at her. Marcella opened her mouth like she was going to say something, but she shut it again. "See you tomorrow, Marcie," Amy whispered, smiling a tiny bit.

Marcella stopped. That is what Amy had always called her. She turned to watch Amy walking away from her, going down the road to go home. "Bye Amy," she said softly before running home. She didn't look back again.

Veronica:

Pirate's Trust

Wow he said he was going to be back in an hour. Nick thought to himself as he finished unloading the last few boxes. The night was growing colder by the minute and Nick found himself shivering into his white shirt.

Nick was just about to give up when he heard a familiar voice call from behind, that sent shivers down his spine.

"Hey Nick, fancy seeing you here."

The cold hard voice belonged to no other than Lerman Obottom, the nastiest pirate in Crystal Cove. The last person he would want to encounter on a cold lonely night.

"Hello Lerman," Nick replied trying to sound brave.

Lerman began to walk forward and Nick caught sight of one of his good friends Tom behind him.

Nick abandoned one of the boxes as they began to slowly advance on him.

Confused, Nick called out to Tom hoping that he could explain what was going on but the old man evilly smiled following the other pirate.

"What's going on?" Nick said shaking with fear.

"We want to get another navigator Nick, if you know what we mean?"

"But I thought we were friends? Nick shouted at Tom.

"Why would you ever trust my words mate?"

"Because—" but Nick found it hard to answer,

"You see, many people here want you gone." Tom continued, "And we can make it look like an accident, oh poor little crew boy met his end in the fierce sea."

Before Nick could talk or contemplate what was going on, Lerman shoved him hard into the wide sea below them.

Nick felt as though he were falling for an eternity, before he felt the cold water prickling his skin like tiny knives. Bobbing in and out of the water he heard the men's laughter carry on. The waves gave no mercy and Nick soon found himself battling to stay afloat, the disgusting sea water finding refuge in his mouth. As Nick fought to swim to the shore he heard the men's voices fading, until they were just echoes in the wind.

Eight hours later...

As soon as he opened his eyes he saw the bright glowing sun, making his eyes see red spots when he set them toward the vast sea in front of him. The sand beneath him felt soft and hot, and there was no breeze to kill the heat that lay about.

His thoughts seemed fuzzy but he felt happy to be alive. As soon as his eyes adjusted to the bright sun he began to go and wander this strange island that he so miraculously landed upon, thanking his lucky stars that the sea had not swallowed him, he began to walk with a skip in his step and determination set on his face.

Not long after Nick stumbled upon a tiny village in the heart of the island, and as he asked around he soon found out that he was in one of the far away islands called Tavern fog. He had heard stories of this place but never ventured far enough to discover the beauty of this small town. The people were nice and hospitable and Nick decided that he would stay in this tiny heaven for awhile before he went back to Crystal Cove, for he had no intention to come face to face with the very people that tried to kill him, Especially Tom.

So as the weeks flew by he decided that he would go back to Crystal Cove to see his family again and trust no one as they could easily betray him, just as Tom had.

León:

All Else Fails

We were walking through the dark street, only illuminated by the darkness of the moon. I thought it was beautiful, the shining moonlight. I could smell various vegetables, from the little restaurant that cooked the best ramen in town. I was silently mortified about what Seikastu and I were doing... it seemed wrong. They told me it was all right; it was for the family

I looked around the street. The darkness illuminated the thoroughfare. I could still smell the soy sauce that is made in the hut just outside the market area.

We walked as quietly as possible through the market area, soon finding the hut that my brother frequented. I took the burlap bags out of my pouch. We soon found the vegetable storage and opened it. We began putting vegetables into the burlap bag we had, filling it halfway so I could carry it. Seikastu put some jars of soy sauce in it; I hung the bag off my shoulder.

I was walking out of the hut, my heavy bag in hand, when a guard spotted me. He shouted at me to stop, so I broke out into a dash, weighed down by my bag I couldn't pick up speed. My legs started burning shortly, I looked back and the guard just passed the hut I just exited, then my brother ran out without his bag...?

What in the?! I thought as I tripped and landed on my gut, knocking the wind out of me, "ugh..."

"Ha! You thought you could run from me you little brat! You'll be serving time for this boy!" he grabbed me by my neck and began leading me out of the marketplace... towards the dungeons....

I was just awaking in the dungeon as my parents were paying off my fines... I could hear my father's discontent voice ringing in my head. I began sobbing; I knew I was in for a lashing. The guard took me out of my cell and led me to my parents. I remember seeing a man in rags in the cell down the hall from mine; I was scared of being here, the rocky surface felt weird underneath my bare feet, and I could smell piss.

I got home and my dad shoved me toward my room, Seikastu was kneeling at the table. He told me

"Be ready to work your ass off."

"You idiot!" He yelled at me, pacing around the room. "You little rat! If you ever do what you did again, you'll be toast! What were you thinking? Trying to get your brother in trouble? Then running off?! You caused a lot of trouble!"

"What?" I screamed as I felt the lightning like lash hit my back. It hurt unlike anything I felt before as the spiny rope struck my back for the second time. To think to open the skin, but I was terrified that it would.

I was so confused after all of it had happened. I was a rat? I tried to get him in trouble? He abandoned me! A million and one thoughts were buzzing in my head as I lay on my stomach, letting my back heal.

At around fifteen lashes—because I counted—my mom came in and stopped him. Apparently Seikastu had become sick, and needed to go to the doctor. Now I was tied onto the bed, trying to relax. I guess trust can be easily lost. I had my ideas.

Emily:

Me, Myself and I

Friday afternoon I found myself sitting alone in a coffee shop, over thinking. Of course. I was waiting for someone: that someone who does not exist. Every day I spend alone, waiting and waiting. What am I waiting for?

I have a loving family, food on the table, clothes to wear. Yet that isn't enough for me to be happy, for me to smile, for me to laugh. I keep my issues to myself mostly because there are people in this world who do not have food, clothes or a family, yet they still smile and laugh. I used to smile, heck, I used to laugh, until one day I was betrayed, betrayed by my only friend. Sad isn't it?

When I was fourteen I was stoked on life. I didn't have friends but I had a best friend and an amazing boyfriend with whom I was head over heels. But enough about him. My best friend and I, we told each other everything. I mean everything. She knew everything about me and I knew everything about her. We shared clothes, makeup, sometimes we'd even switch dogs for a day (shhh my parents still don't know). But one day everything changed, we didn't share clothes we didn't laugh we didn't even have conversation. "I asked her what was wrong, why she wouldn't talk or look at me, she replied with." "I just want to be alone right now." I said "okay." I mean everyone has those days. But no, not us. We'd always talk to each other when we're feeling down so I started to question myself.

Later that day I spotted her' she was crying. "I went up to her asked what was wrong again and then my heart stopped. Not literally. She told me she slept with my boyfriend." I was speechless, this rage inside of me was telling me to forgive and forget but what am I showing myself? What would I be showing my parents and siblings? That I have no respect for myself. That day my best friend and I did not talk again, we didn't laugh, we didn't share our dogs. My boyfriend and I didn't have sleepovers, or have the "I love you more" fights. That day I disappeared.

Four months later I was diagnosed with depression and anorexia. I'm homeschooled now. It sounds stupid I know a break up effects your mental health. What a loser right?

I'm sixteen now and I fell in love; I didn't know I could ever love someone again, mostly because I don't. I fell in love with myself.

Tristyn:

Trust Can Be Lost in Seconds

"John! Stop!"

John turned around to his best friend James running down the hallway.

"Guess what?" James panted

John just shrugged his shoulders, "What?"

"There's is a party tonight. You wanna go?"

"No, not really. I have a lot of homework I gotta do tonight

"Come on" James cajoled. You will have fun we haven't partied together in forever. Just come out, you won't regret it."

"OK, OK" John said. "I will come. What time?"

"We are leaving at 10 I will be outside your house."

"Ok I will see you then," just then the bell rang.

"Oh well I gotta go to class I will see you later" James said. "You won't regret it!"

As John walked in the door of the house, after school he took his shoes off at the door and puts them on the shoe rack. He went upstairs and dropped his bag by the couch.

"Hey Dad, could I go to a party tonight?"

His dad asked, "Whose party, what time, when would you get home, and do you have any homework?"

John grinned. "A friend's, 10, and um, I'm not sure, and no I don't."

"No. You can't go tonight."

"That's not fair!"

"Life isn't fair, son."

John stomped to his room.

John flopped onto his bed. *I'm just gonna sneak out and my Dad won't notice I'm gone* at ten o'clock he crept out his bedroom door, and hear his dad snoring. He tiptoed to the front door. James was waiting.

"Okay. Let's do this, John."

They started walking to the party. After an hour they arrived at the drive way of this HUGE HOUSE. John smiles at James, "Let's party"

John felt his heart beat very quickly, as he entered the house. His Dad will check on him? John went to James. "I'm not feeling good I thinking I'm heading home."

If his dad found out that he'd snuck out, he would be in trouble. He started to jog a little down the street, then that jog turned into a run and that run turned into a full sprint he made it home twenty minutes.

He was too late. His dad was sitting in a chair waiting for him to get home.

"Where have you been?"

"I went to that party that I wasn't allowed to."

The little vein in his dad's forehead was getting bigger and bigger. *One of these times it will pop*, John thought

"How long should you be grounded for?"

"I don't know."

You won't like how long I will ground you for."

Trust can be lost in seconds

It will happen again

Cydney:

The Cat Life.

"Hey Buddy!" I meowed from across the living room.

Buddy's ears perked up and turned to me. "Hey Bridget!" He got up and trotted over to me in that odd doggy way, with his long golden fur shining in the small patch of sunlight coming from the big living room window.

"Want to play a game of hide and seek?"

"You're obviously going to win because cats are much stealthier than dogs" Buddy rolled his eyes and lay down on his pillow.

"Who's here?" I purred as I heard a knock on the door.

"BARK! BARK! BARK!" Buddy started going crazy at the knock of the door which is very out of character for him.

"Hey there, Bridge and Bud," our owner said as he stroked Buddy's head.

Buddy followed our owner into the kitchen. "BAD DOG! GET OUT!" our owner yelled.

Buddy sadly walked out of the kitchen and lay down on his bed.

"What's wrong Buddy?" I meowed as I stretched.

"I got yelled at," Buddy whimpered.

Buddy put his head down and drifted off to sleep.

Off in dreamland...

"Buddy! Want to play chase the squirrel?"

"Sure!"

Buddy and Bridget ran outside to middle of the yard to listen for squirrels

"There's one! Get It" Buddy barked.

"First one to it wins" Bridget hissed

They raced to the squirrel, faster and faster Buddy charged towards the squirrel!

But at the last second, as Bridget was sprinting to it, gripping the ground with her claws, she leaped forwards, tackling the squirrel with all her strength.

Buddy, not far behind her, barking like crazy.

"Bridget! Stop! You're hurting it!"

She looked at the squirrel, so innocent, no defense whatsoever.

"I...I...I'm sorry..." Bridget meowed as she walked away slowly.

Waking up...

"Buddy? Buddy! Wake up!"

"Huh?! What?!" Buddy said as if he had just seen a ghost.

"You started whimpering in your sleep!"

"Oh..."

"Anyway, I wanted to know if you wanted to play chase the squir----"

"NO!" Buddy growled as he cut me off.

"Um...Okay?" I meowed walking to my water bowl.

I knew that something was not right with Buddy.

"Buddy, what's wrong?"

"Would you ever hurt a poor defenseless animal, Bridget?"

"Why do you ask?"

"Just wondering"

"...okay...anyway...want to go play outside?" I purred.

"Sure"

Buddy and I lay down on the front lawn in the sunlight.

"Look Buddy! A Bird!' I meowed

"Wow!" He woofed.

"Be right back!"

"Ok?"

I quietly stalk the bird, watching it's every move. I slowly make my way towards it, it's now time to catch my prey.

I pounce on the bird, holding it captive in my mouth.

"BRIDGET STOP!!!!!!!!" Buddy barked over and over again.

I looked at Buddy, and put the bird down, and watched it fly away.

"Why are you stopping me, Bud?"I said wondering why he was stopping me.

"Because you shouldn't hurt poor defenseless animals!!"

"It's the cycle of life! Jeez!" I hissed.

"I trusted you wouldn't hurt an animal!"

"What do you mean?"

"If you hurt or kill animals, then how can I trust you? You might hurt me…"

"Buddy I would never hurt you!"

"Then promise me you won't hurt another animal."

"Ok, I promise."

We decide to go back inside and eat dinner, chicken and kibble.

"Be right back!" I meowed.

"Ok" Buddy woofed.

I walked outside for some fresh air; I can smell the pine trees surrounding the house.

Then all of a sudden, I hear a squeak. The squeak of a mouse.

Don't do it. You promised Buddy.

I am so tempted to kill that mouse.

I gave in.

I pounced on the mouse, killing it from fright, and all I heard was a soft whimper from behind me…

"I trusted you…"

Tiffany:

Friendship Is Nothing Without Trust

I walked down the halls with my friend Tina, both of us hoping not to get trampled by the rush of people trying to go for lunch. When we had gotten closer to our lockers Tina stopped and turned toward me. "I'm going to run to the bathroom. I'll be really quick so we can go for lunch."

"Okie doke." I responded trying to open my stubborn lock. I opened the door, at last, into the silence of the suddenly empty halls. I heard footsteps echoing off the walls and turned around to call to Tina. "Hey, you were really qui-" I froze mid sentence, my mouth dropped open.

"Hey!" Jessica flipped her long golden hair off her shoulder, and her gorgeous blue eyes sparkled as she batted her long eyelashes.

I looked down the hall way to see who she is talking to. "Ya, I'm talking you. You're Clare right?" Jessica giggled.

Why is she staring at me like that? I wondered. Until I realized I had just been standing there with my mouth open after she asked me who I was. "Uh… ya." I should have said something cooler. I'm an idiot.

"Ok sweet. So, anyhow, I've noticed you around school and thought you seemed pretty cool," Jessica started smiling like a cat. "I thought maybe we could hang out for lunch?"

"Sure." I turned to compose my face as I put my books into my locker. *I can't believe she thinks I'm "cool"*. I turn back to Jessica and close the door, fully in control of myself again.

Jessica flashed her white teeth. "That's great!" Her smile faded to a look of concern. "You weren't hoping to have that weird Tina girl come, were you? 'Cause she's kind of a freak."

"No, of course not! We aren't even really friends, I just hang out with her because I feel bad for her." I lied like a mad man. "She doesn't really have many friends. Probably because she is fourteen and still sleeps with a teddy bear and her baby blanket." I sputtered, after just telling my best friends biggest secret. I could feel my chest tighten, as if a huge weight had just been sent on it.

"Oh, wow, she is a freak." Jessica started giggling. "It's a good thing that you guys aren't actually friends though right? 'Cause I'm pretty sure she just heard everything you just said." Pointing behind me, Jessica had begun laughing harder.

I turned around, to see Tina standing just far enough down the hallway to have heard everything. Tears streamed down her face. "I told you that, believing you wouldn't say anything to anyone else. You were supposed to be my best friend, I trusted you!" The tears were coming down harder with every word she said. "But I guess we aren't friends though, right? I'm just the freak with no one, except for you, the one who just pretends to be my friend." She turned and dashed back down the hall toward the bathroom.

Tears were building up in my eyes and I began to tremble as I turned to look back at Jessica.

"Well, that was entertaining!" Jessica looped her arm into my trembling one. "Good thing you guys weren't friends."

"Not anymore." The tears in my eyes were burning, threatening to escape. I should be happy right now. I'm going to be friends with Jessica. So why do I feel like I just made the biggest mistake I've ever made?

Bethany:

Shattered Glass

Trust is something you give to people right? You expect them to keep it. In my sixteen years of living I've had many times where I have trusted people and they didn't keep it. October 15th 2008, for example I was eight years old, I remember my dad walking through the door, home from work like every other day.

"Daddy's home!" I ran to the door, giving him a big bear hug.

"Hi Olive." He gave me a kiss on my cheek.

"Hi darling" my mother came in and gave him a kiss on the cheek; a smile filled her face.

"Hello Crystal" his face was blank like seeing her meant nothing.

I ran back up to my bedroom and continued playing with my Barbies.

"How was your day?" she sat on the couch

"What's it to you?" He walked over to the fridge and grabbed a beer.

"I was just asking how your day was; I'm your wife." She sighed pressing her hand over her forehead.

"It was good. Went to the Pub with some of my buddies." He sipped his beer, staring at the ceiling avoiding eye contact with her.

"Are you serious? Weren't they expecting you at work today?" she clenched her fists, her heart beating faster. "Do you not understand that there are bills to be paid? Our daughter to take care of? My job at the bank is only two days a week; I don't get enough to support us."

"You are making a big deal out of this! It's one day!!" he slammed his bottle on the top of the side table.

"You don't understand, this is a big deal because it's unprofessional. You could lose your job, you can't expect them to let you skip work anytime you want, they could fire you."

"I'VE HAD ENOUGH OF YOUR JUDGEMENT! YOU ARENT THE ONE WORKING EVERY FLIPPEN DAY TO PAY SOME STUPID BILLS" he stood up went to the fridge again grabbing but another drink. He stumbled over to her.

"Get out of here you jerk! You're drunk! Get out of here." She cried kneeling on the ground, weeping.

He left, slamming the door behind him; I heard it and ran down stairs to see what was up.

At 12pm that night my dad showed up again, he smelt of liquor, the smell was nauseating. "GIVE YOUR DAD A HUG!" he screamed walking towards me

My mom pulled me away.

After I refused that hug he got angry, so angry. He didn't touch me though; he blamed it all on momma. "You're a worthless piece of $@#*!!! Let her go! She's my daughter too!!!"

He yelled and all I could hear was the shattering of a beer bottle and my mother's scream. I ran to the phone screaming and unable to breathe I was in shock, I quickly called 911. Mother laid on the floor passed out, my father continued to curse at her and I was on the phone "Olive Grace Bowmen" he said slurring his words and racing towards me, he came and grabbed me pinning in the corner of the kitchen. "WHY YOU CALLING THE POLICE?!!"

That was a night I will remember forever, I think it has personally changed me in bad ways and some good. Trust is something I treasure and take very seriously now. I trusted my dad not to hurt my mom and me, but he did. We can't change the past or his decisions, but we can change our decisions and the way we look at life and when and whom we trust.

Jade:

Played

Some might say they were the closest friends in school, until the fighting had started, the jealousy began. High school is nerve wracking enough and it's even worse when there is so much drama going on that you actually feel physically sick to your stomach, whether you are included in it or not. This story is going to sound a lot like the sappy ones where the guy gets the girl and the best friend is forgotten. That's not exactly how this one goes.

It was the first day of high school, the two best friends were roaming the halls of the old run down high school they have been attending to since grade nine. The walls had the paint chipped off and the lockers spray painted. Of course Madison's tag-along boyfriend tagged along. Bianca always became the third wheel. Madison and Bianca, these two had been inseparable since pre-school, and their parents had been the best of friends since their days in high school. Wesley and Madison had been together a lot lately so Bianca had to find new people to hang out with, until she got a call from Madison.

"Wes and I just broke up. He said we were getting to be old news,"

Bianca's face went still; everyone had always thought that those two would be together till graduation.

Bianca looked Madison's teary eyed face, "It's okay. He was a jerk."

"Thanks B. You always know how to make me feel better."

After the blow up between Wes and Madison, Wes started luring Bianca in with his stupid games and you could tell Madison wasn't happy about it just by the way she acted, with her long hair always tied back and that look in her eyes. Wes walked up to them in the cafeteria and sat beside Bianca.

Madison gave her the 'look.' The look of madness glowed through her hazel brown eyes. Bianca quivered with worry.

Wes put his arm around Bianca "Hey guys no need for things to get tense; I'm just coming to say hi."

Madison got up and stormed away with her hair swishing back and forth. Bianca turned to Wes.

"Are you serious? I know you don't actually like me and you're only doing this to make Madison jealous." It was working; you could see her pissed off face coming from a mile away. Bianca knew she and Madison were not friends any more especially when Madison stormed up to her in her heels so she hovered above her. She started screaming while waving her arms around almost smacking Madison in the face. BOOM! Bianca slapped Madison in her perfectly contoured face. Wes came running up to them, grabbed Bianca's quivering hands and walked down the dark hallway looking back constantly. Madison's face went red with anger; she stormed off smacking and shaking the lockers on her way. Bianca was in shock she didn't know what was going on.

She had left Wes; she couldn't handle any more feud with Madison. She texted Madison that night

"I'm sorry Madison, we really need to talk."

"Yes we do, and I'm sorry too"

"I think we both need to get over him"

"Yeah I'm done with his crap, it's over."

"Agreed."

Nicole:

Not Everyone Values Your Trust

Ever notice how bad moments normally happen in slow motion so you get to soak in every single dreadful detail? Even though you wouldn't ever want to be a part of that moment, you are. You may want to just disappear, get away from this as quickly as possible; but you don't because unfortunately. You didn't get accepted into Hogwarts and you don't have that invisible cloak. You are most certainly there, clear as day, pale faced, cold to the touch with that disgusting feeling in your very own stomach.

That's exactly how Isabella felt as she watched Luke from across the club slobbering all over the red head with the obviously fake super model body. She wouldn't cry over this of course; tears are the number one public display of weakness. Plus, she had watched him do this many times; they had been dating ever since they were sixteen and it had been on and off. It hadn't ever really been a loving relationship, but for some reason he always ended up going straight back to her and for some sick reason she always accepted him back with open arms.

But this time it was different, Isabella wasn't going to just stand there and wait for him to come back.

She slammed back her last shot of whiskey, grabbed her purse and told her friends that she would text them the next morning. She glanced over at Luke and the redhead only to see that his eyes were watching her cross the room, she flicked her attention back to the exit and closed the door to the back alley with a loud slam. She knew he would follow. He always did and that's exactly what she wanted. She was extremely satisfied with the sound of his expensive shoes hitting the pavement behind her.

"Bella, where are you going?" The low grumble in his voice which she had once fallen for now made her skin crawl with annoyance.

"I'm going home." She sighed with a shrug and kept walking.

"No, you're not." He grabbed her by the waist and roughly threw her against the wall. This wasn't very unusual, but it still shocked her every time he would act out violently.

"Yes, I am." She informed him as she steadied herself and shoved him away. "I'm done dealing with you. You're like a child and honestly I'm *sick* of you. I've watched you be unfaithful for years and I forgave you every single time, but I'm done being the good person who just lies down and gets walked all over, while you get your way with everything."

He laughed humorlessly, which would have been terrifying for any other person but to Isabella it was a sign of fear. She stared intensely while his eyes darted around the alley looking like a trapped animal and she just smirked coldly back at this behavior.

"I'll be better. Isabelle please don't do this. You can't just leave me, Bella."

"Oh, but trust me. I am." She continued to smile dangerously watching the terror in his crawl into his disturbed blue eyes as she pulled her hand gun out of her purse and pulled the trigger.

As he dropped to the ground a sleek black car pulled into the alley; two men in black suits proceeded get out of the car and dropped him into the trunk after binding his hands together. She shot Luke once more with the tranquillizer, just to make sure he slept nicely.

"Sleep well, my love." She giggled wickedly and slammed the trunk shut.

Creative Writing Class

Story excerpts

Autumn:

Eyland is an incomplete fifteen thousand world young adult novella. Ailleen runs away from her destiny as a sacrifice to the gods and must survive against the odds in an ancient Norse forest.

Eyeland

Aileen jogged swiftly across the damp, bouncy forest floor. It was a rainforest, so the air was thick with humidity.

She was completely silent, only the sound of her breath and the quiet rush of water was to be heard.

She was on a mission today, a large patch of salmon berries would be at the peak of their ripeness. Aileen found that, when this happened last year and she was late, the Bears and other forest creatures had eaten every last one. Which rendered her starved and desperate, she was forced to eat mice and any other small rodent that came her way. So she told herself that she would have to get there early next year. And early she was, based on her makeshift sundial, it was five in the morning, the sun was barely up.

She used her silver dagger to rip through a patch of tall grass, and the clearing came into view. It was a beautiful day, so the early morning sun shone throughout the forest canopy.

A smile spread across Aileen's face as she looked down and saw the, ripe, red berries.

Aileen tossed her bow and arrow aside.

She smiled, her misfortune was over now, and she would no longer be hungry.

Aileen guessed that the reason she couldn't find food was because she had somehow angered the land spirits. Perhaps by overconsumption of trees, or not enough sacrifices. Whatever the reason, her dry spell was officially over.

Aileen looked at the thorny branches that protected the berries. She had to get them somehow, without the spines getting in her skin and causing an itchy rash. She thought on this for a moment and came up with a solution. She pulled out her leather satchel and tied it to a strong stick. She pushed the satchel against the bush and the berries fell gently into her bag. She had done this once before, when her pa had ordered her to go and pick some berries for breakfast.

Aileen's pa was tough; it seemed as though there no shred of decency or sensitivity in his body. He pillaged, stole, and raided monasteries. But that's usual for most Vikings. He once told Aileen to kill a nest of baby birds because they were getting on his nerves and he wanted her to see death and become numb to it. No matter how much she cried and cried, he made her smash the nest under a boulder. She was six at the time.

Aileen pulled her satchel off of the stick, and shoved a few berries into her mouth, they were delicious! She wiped the sticky red juice off of her face.

She wanted to eat more, but she closed her satchel. She had to offer the rest to Freya, the goddess of crops and plants. Aileen was a pagan, so she had multiple gods that required multiple sacrifices and offerings of different kinds.

It was a long walk back to her spot in the woods. See lived in a hammock that was suspended between two trees, with a canvas tarp draped over it in the branches above to keep her dry. Next to that, she had her sundial, her fire pit, her axe, and pile of firewood that she kept dry with a piece of leather that she draped over top.

She flipped her long, silvery hair out of her eyes and crawled over some large red wood that had fallen in the last huge storm. They kept a lot of the wind off of her and proved to be useful, they were filled with grubs and worms that could be eaten in times of desperation.

Aileen had inherited most of her ma's looks like her small nose, her fair skin, and her rounded face. But she had her dad's cold, ice-blue eyes. Her small figure allowed her to move swiftly and silently through the woods.

She looked down at her necklace of sacrifice and sighed. It was a painful and constant reminder of her selfish mistake.

Back in her old town Osomi, a drought was happening. So Aileen's pa (who was the Jarl, the leader of the town.) decided that he was much too important to be sacrificed, so he offered Aileen to take his place. She was forced accept. Half the town crammed in to two longboats and set sail to a nearby temple. But before that could get there, deep in the night, Aileen snuck onto a small boat in the middle of the night. And drove it from the longship that she was placed on, to a remote island that she had heard stories about. Pagans called the island; "Eyland of Fenrir" meaning "island of the wolf."

This was a serious offence to the gods, so Aileen was punished with little food and a spell of dry weather. But somehow, she survived. Of course, not without the occasional fight for her life now and then. Just last week, she had to kill a huge wolf with her bow and arrow.

Aileen looked down at her firewood pile and sighed. Her supply was dangerously low. So she picked up her axe and went to look for some dry wood. And a few minutes later, she came back with an arm full of perfectly cut wood.

She laid it down and pulled out her necklace. She placed it on a stump and placed a wax candle next to it.

This was Aileen's way of offering things to the gods. She pulled out her satchel and spread some berries in front of her shrine.

"Perfect!" She smiled and stood back to admire her handiwork.

"Ugh" she muttered as she looked at her sundial, the day was barely over yet. She hadn't a thing to do.

Aileen wandered through the forest, by now the sun was half up and the birds were singing their loud, yet lovely song.

She began to wonder if she would be here forever. Would she starve to death? Or get eaten by an animal? She started to wonder about her aunt Zelda, and her mother Cloe. They were her two closest friends, when it came down to it. When Aileen was a child, she never really was one for playing outside so she spent most of her time with her mom and aunt. Cleaning, cooking, and milking the cows.

Time seemed to go quickly when Aileen became lost in her thoughts.

Then it was nearly night.

So she lit a fire, and lay down on her hammock. Sleep came slowly; she kept hearing noises outside…

León:

Samurai Beat is an incomplete ten thousand word young adult fantasy novella. During sixteenth century Japan, Rayal, a young Samurai leader, is forced to battle his brother to avenge the death of their mother.

Samurai Beat

"Hmm?" I looked at my desk, it was filled with drawings and documents concerning my little village; the village of Sana. I stood up, and pulled my long black hair off of my sweaty neck. I fixed my kimono, and slipped on my sandals.

I sat down and grabbed my paint brush, and began writing on a piece of paper; only a few moments later one of my senior spies busted into my room, exasperated and sweaty, "huff, huff- Rayal... the elves... are planning a huge attack...." He said, grasping his chest in pain. A worried face contorted with pain.

"What?!" I shot up from my chair and it crashed on the ground, "When? Why? We aren't ready for this!"

"Well," Barge – my father - waited a minute to catch his breath; "I had finally found a good vantage point, and was looking down into... his room," he said spitefully his brow wrinkling in anger and his hands clenching, apparently remembering an old failure "and I saw all the plans.... they said around the beginning of fall... Rayal, and they want it quick."

"But it's mid-spring... why wait that long?"

"Because of resources, after summer, all crops have been harvested, and it gives them a long time to prepare routes, camps, and siege machines."

"Siege machines? We only have eight foot wooden walls! They could scale them easily!"

"Just a thought, calm down, you always have been quite literal." He said mockingly

"Oh…" I sat back down, quite hurt by his comment "Okay…well than what we shall do? We would have to build better defenses." I started to envision: bigger and better walls, a powerful army, it was all possible! I fell into a slight trance remembering everything my brother Seikastu had done to me…

* * *

We were walking through the dark street, only illuminated by the darkness of the moon. I thought it was beautiful, the shining moonlight. I could smell various vegetables, from the little restaurant that cooked the best ramen in town. I was silently mortified about what Seikastu and I were doing… it seemed wrong. They told me it was all right, it was for the family

I looked around the street. The darkness illuminated the thoroughfare. I could still smell the soy sauce that is made in the hut just outside the market area. Best in the village, specially made for the order; I liked the slightly salted.

We walked as quietly as possible through the market area, soon finding the hut that my brother frequented. I always wondered how we were getting food. I took the burlap bags out of my pouch at my waist. We soon found the vegetable storage and opened it. We began putting vegetables into the burlap bag we had, filling it halfway so I could carry it. Seikastu put some jars of soy sauce in it; I hung the bag off my shoulder.

I was walking out of the hut, my heavy bag in hand, when a guard spotted me. He shouted at me to stop, so I broke out into a dash; weighed down by my bag I couldn't pick up speed. I looked back and the guard just passed the hut I just exited, then my brother ran out without his bag.

What in the-?! I thought as I tripped and landed on my gut, knocking the wind out of me, "Ugh…"

"Ha! You thought you could run from me you little brat! You'll be serving time for this boy!" He grabbed me by my neck squeezing hard and began leading me out of the marketplace towards the dungeons….

I was just awakening in the dungeon as my parents were paying off my fines… I could hear my father's discontented voice ringing in my head. I began sobbing; it was obvious that I was in for a lashing. The guard took me out of my cell and led me down the hall towards my parents. I remember seeing a man in rags in the cell down the hall from mine, his thinning by the hour. I was scared of being here, the rocky surface felt weird underneath my bare feet, and I could smell piss.

I got home and my dad shoved me toward my room. Seikastu was kneeling at the table.

"Be ready to work your butt off." He told me.

"You idiot!" He yelled at me, pacing around the room. "You little rat! If you ever do what you did again, you'll be toast! What were you thinking? Trying to get your brother in trouble? Then running off?! You caused a lot of trouble!"

"What?" I screamed as I felt the lightning like lash hit my back.

"We have to strike first!" I yelled,

"How? How is our little village supposed to march up the mountains and challenge the elves? Be smart young one, because we are the only ones you got! We must fortify the fort and wait in preparation."

"Barge…" I took a deep breath, "even if we fortify the fort, they have the high ground. They have enough power in one man to defeat half of our army. Their fort is in an indefensible location; we would have a much better advantage. Please agree with me, because if you don't I'll be stuck to continue without the blessing of my father. Please father, believe me, this is the only way we will win."

"Okay… I guess this could work. But we must recruit more soldiers. Our military is only 250 strong, at most." He spat out the words like sunflower seeds.

"That is no problem; we could get over a thousand recruits! You know the other villages owe us. They would have no choice but to give us recruits. But you must promise that there will be no children. Please, no others should be put through what I had to do, okay?"

"Al-… all right, no children, give me an age restriction," he demanded bitterly.

"Let's say… eighteen. Will that work?"

"Yes… it'll work." He walked out of the room.

***

I walked through the village, already late for the first training session. I got to the training grounds and took my station at the lead of quadrant one… well the only quadrant now, but as soon as more recruits entered the military, we would have four quadrants.

I began with the art of blade dancing, easily lining up with the rest.

***

"Everyone!" I shouted across the broad training ground, "There are four squad leaders, water, fire, air, and earth, if you have that symbol, than find your leader!" after about ten minutes, they had all crowded into their squads.

"Your squad leaders will give you assignments; you will either be sparring, digging, or any task your squad leader gives you! Commence!"

As they all filed out of the training grounds, I left to watch the sparring.

As I got into the dojo, I noticed four different spars had already commenced. Then I saw one new recruit had whacked his opponent, flipping him on his butt. I continued to walk over, grabbed a kendo stick, and walked into the sparring ring. We must have been one or two years apart in age, so I figured it would be all right.

"Ready your weapon," I said warningly, "this is not going to be an easy fight for you."

I raised my weapon in a Kenjutsu pose, similar to the Dai techniques.

"Hrrrragh!" I yelled as I made a sweeping downwards strike, then mid swing he raised his sword, I swung my sword to the right, down to his ankles and hooked his foot, pulling my sword towards me causing him to fall on his butt.

"Preying on the weak, and underestimating the strong. You are an unintelligent pig. I had high expectations for you." I spat in disgust and walk out of the dojo.

* * *

"Thank you all for being here," I said, bowing graciously. "It is an honor for the wise council to meet at such short notice, but this situation is dire…." I took a small breath, and started explaining the fact that the elves were readying for the march in the fall.

"If we strike first, we have a chance! You must agree, right?"

"Mhm…" the eldest in the council cleared his throat, "Well… it's almost time for my meditating, so shall we vote for Rayal's idea? All in favor?"

"Aye!" the room chanted.

"Then we shall crush our enemies under our heels, and make Seikastu pay for the pain he has caused this village!"

"Aye!" They all chanted.

* * *

I was in my bedroom lying on my bed mat. I couldn't stop thinking about my sparring match from earlier. Would he quit? I hope he grows from that experience. I got up from my bed and walked to my wardrobe, took out my favorite kimono—the one with the cherry blossoms—and began walking out of my room. I put the kimono on, loosely enough that I could walk around comfortably within my home.

I walked into the main portion of my home and grabbed my kendo stick. I began twirling it in my hand. It was short and old. I received the kendo stick when I was only eleven years old. My father had given it to me when I was to start training for Advanced Samurai Cavalry unit. He also gave me a small pony, just a year old.

I looked out my window at my horse. He was black and white, an average colored horse in this village. He was getting older, but still faithful, I had broken him early, with the help of my father, and he's always been good for rides, a gentle horse, but not a battle horse.

Thinking back to my childhood I remembered the bumps and bruises I received from my training, always hoping it would lead to my betterment, it did… but at the expense of my family. But it's too beautiful of a day to be bringing myself down.

I put on my Hakama and walked out of the house. I walked to my stable and saddled my horse. I led him out into the openness. I mounted him and began riding out eastwards; it was a beautiful day, not to be wasted.

I topped the hill and looked down on the training grounds, wondering. I could see the top of one of the dojos. I decided to go and see how many new recruits we had.

After a short canter through the training ground I arrived at the barracks, I tethered my horse and walked inside.

"Good afternoon and how are you, Whistler."

"Hello, Rayal. Why may I ask, are you here?" They bowed,

"Well, if you wouldn't mind, I would like to know how many recruits have we received from our neighbors?"

"Erg-hem," He cleared his throat, and grabbed a couple documents; "We have received over a thousand, five hundred from the nearest empire village, Kurokku machi. They seem eager to help our village."

"Okay..." I thought about that, "Are they here?"

"Ha," He scoffed, "Not for a week."

"All right, well, I'll be off. Thank you Whistler,"

"Mhm," He hummed in response.

I walked out of the barracks and hopped back onto my horse. I was off to the southern wall, curious if the five hundred new soldiers were in sight.

I got to the southern wall. It was an eight-foot-or-so wooden post wall, sturdy enough to hold back most humans.

I hopped off my horse

The guards walked into the tower with the geared mechanism. They turned the crank until the gate opened.

I walked through the gate and surveyed the area around me. There was a dense forest to the west, a cobblestone path towards the north. I spied across the land, looking for any signs of a group, or a camp. After a little bit of looking, I saw a man on a horse, it didn't look like a soldier though, more like a... Ronin.

I retreated inside the gates and grabbed a weapon, a Dai Katana, and placed the sword over my shoulder.

I re-exited the gate, and walked several feet down the path. I looked towards my surroundings. It was an open area, probably one hundred feet of crowning hills, somewhat beautiful, except the barren hill tops and burnt crests. Then my eyes drifted towards the training fields, completely trampled, even though they were not often used. The stray horseman was crossing the trampled and barren training fields, obviously traveling towards my village. He would be there in about quarter of an hour. I crossed my arms. I kicked some pebbles away from me, but soon there was nothing left to kick, and the horseman was still only halfway here.

I started to pace towards the forest, doubling back towards the top of the hill. Almost cresting it was my dear cousin Rinku.

"Rinku! My cousin, what brings you to my home? I thought you were a Ronin!"

"Well, cousin, I received word that my oldest cousin was bullying the little runt again. I decided to come on down and protect him."

"Oh Rinku, it's so nice to see you again. Come, we can have tea."

"That sounds like a fine idea."

We walked towards the gate, looking at the walls I thought *if anybody knows how to reinforce walls it's-*

"Your walls are puny. We must make them bigger!"

"I know, Rinku."

"You should know better! Seikastu would scale these walls without a sweat!"

"But," I was obviously flustered by his accusations, "I... I know Rinku."

"We shall make you grand walls, with a forest just down the hill to us. Rayal, we have much to talk about before we begin upgrading these walls." He said as we walked beyond the gate.

Rinku hopped down from his horse and gave it to the stable-boy.

"Actually, we have quite the journey, all the way across the village to my hut. Keep your horse until we get to my home."

"I want to call that wise, but I would much rather be next to the main gate if I was you."

We hopped onto our horses and cantered through the village, only stopping at the training grounds to watch over the sparring briefly.

We got to my house shortly after that. I put some water in my kettle, and got the green tea out.

"Living in style my cousin, different than before, eh?"

"Oh yes, Rinku. I sometimes feel out of place in this hut."

"I would too, it's big! You have an oven! How did you get all the clay to make that? I barely have a hearth."

"The river; it contains glacial water, so it's pure, and contains a lot of clay."

"Maybe I will need to take some home with me."

"Feel free, we have more than enough."

I watched him look around, obviously out of his element. I sniffed the tea, it smelled of roses. My tea is made of camellia leaves and rose hips, good for memory.

I looked around, listening to the birds chirp outside. I turned my attention back to Rinku. He was relaxing a bit, drinking his tea eagerly.

"Ah, you make good tea. What is it made of little cousin?"

"Well, its basic green tea, mixed with some rose hips, to give it the sweetness. We don't have a lot of sugar, and use most of it in the sake."

"How is your sake?"

"Oh my cousin, it is the best liquor in central Japan!"

"Why am I drinking tea then? We should celebrate my coming with much sake."

"Oh, we shall celebrate my cousin, but not until after the evening hours, and late into the night."

I walked out of my dwelling, and strode towards the house down the street to the celebration supervisor.

I was walking up to the door when it slid open, and Drake exited.

"Why hello, Drake! How go the preparations for our festival tonight?" I asked politely

"Well, we are only slightly behind schedule, but it's making great progress."

"Ah, well, we have an unexpected guest, and would like for an extra keg of sake to be arranged. Also if it's possible, a nice sized boar please."

"Well, yes... I guess that's possible.

"Thank you. Good friend."

I began walking back towards my house, and I saw Rinku walking, almost pacing, along the street.

"Why are you outside my cousin? You should be inside enjoying our tea!" I called out to him.

"Because, it's a beautiful day little one. We should be enjoying the sun."

"All right, let us go to the ramen shop, free ramen for you, cousin."

"Sounds like an idea."

We grabbed our horses and left.

I was walking down the street attracting the looks of men and women from the village. They were all looking at my cousin and me. I always received looks, mostly due to my long black hair, and my always exposed arms, but also my cousin, who had short blonde hair, and many white man features. His parents were my aunt and a white man, who came to this country unwelcome and unwanted and fell in love with my aunt. It was quite a cute story.

His jaw was always set and his chest was always puffed out. He looked like a stereotypical white sailor. Irony is he did work for the docks all his life.

More and more people were looking at my cousin, uneasy around a white man, even if he was only half a white man. But other ladies where immediately attracted to him, I could tell because he was obviously trying to look good, and only did that when ladies where showing off for him.

"You tease."

"I only tease when being teased little one."

I looked him up and down, admitting to myself he was a handsome man. His gut was flat, which was rare for a white man his age... from the stories I've heard. His hair was always sharp looking; he combed it he told me. His arms were more muscular than mine, which was rare around these parts. It was only because when I moved and worked on the docks with him though, he naturally had muscular arms.

"We are nearing the fair grounds. It may be awkward, but just stand in the front of the crowd. Everyone will clue in to who you are."

"All right. But what about the ramen shop?"

"Would you have followed if I told you we were going to a celebration? With half the village?"

"If you told me there was food, I probably would!"

"All right." I said trying to calm him.

* * *

I was walking up the few stairs to the podium. The stairs were decorated, ready for a celebration with our finest dragon cloth. I could feel the fabric under my hand as I grasped the hand rail.

I glanced down quickly and spotted Rinku. He was as tense as a spruce tree in still wind.

"Rinku, be easy! My people will not hurt you. You are a friend." I said finally boarding the podium. "Friends, Family, we are all here today, for the celebration of our newly arrived friend, Rinku! The best boat builder in the whole of southern Japan, the thickest arms of all Japan, and my greatest cousin."

"We will all go feast until our bellies expand, and the itis puts us to sleep."

The small crowd cheered and began filing towards the feasting area, separated because of the huge smoke house, and the fire pit.

I was walking back down the small staircase, and saw Rinku waiting for me at the bottom.

"Well cousin, have you been welcomed by our village?" I asked politely

"Well... I struck up a conversation with a rather short man, said he was a farmer."

"Short farmer, narrows it down a lot, eh?" I asked sarcastically, "He didn't give you a name?"

"No... nobody has given me a name Rayal; nobody wants me here."

"Hm... well that will change. This village isn't as prejudiced as the rest of this country. I will give it a week.

"Hmph," he scoffed, "I have been given a better reaction than most times. I guess ... it may just be weird moving from one city that had finally accepted me, and another, where I have to start from scratch."

"Yes..."

We began walking towards the feasting grounds, as I quickened my pace, Rinku head hanging, followed at a meager pace, obviously saddened.

As we arrived to the feast, I looked around, trying to find faces as we walked through the slow paced crowd. After a while, I became impatient used my veto to walk up to the front of the line. I got to my seat at the head of the table. I stood up at the back of the chair, began looking around and saw Rinku conversing with a shorter man, a smile stretched across my face due to the fact that Rinku was fitting in better than even I thought.

I sat down as the crowd thinned and almost everyone was seated. It was almost time to feast and I could tell everyone was getting anxious.

"Well my fellow people, let us feast until our bellies expand!" I announced raising my arms high in earnest.

"Aye!" the entire crowd cheered.

As I was eating meagerly, I looked around for the sake barrels. I could tell that everybody was drinking due to the fact that, in not ten minutes, two full barrels of sake had been tapped and drank. I finally looked around to spot Rinku, and finally spotted him after his thunderous laugh attracted my attention.

Then finally everybody turned their heads up to the stage, as our performers began to announce their acts.

"Welcome to the festival that we have created to commemorate the arrival of Rinku, the strongest engineer in all of Japan!" The performer stopped and let the crowd cheer "And now, our strongest performers, will perform Ame to kaminari no dansu; The Dance of Rain and Thunder!" The crowd cheered once again, but where soon muted by the ominous blowing of horns introducing the dancers. Then the plucking of Junanagan, strumming the likeliness of rain as the dancers danced.

Boom! The drum thundered, as the dancers froze, **Boom!** The drum thundered once again, and the dancers resumed.

* * *

Just as the festival was thinning out and lamps were dying, I saw Rinku fast approaching, a smile from ear to ear, as his mother would say.

"Thank you Rayal. This has been a wonderful experience! I had my doubts, but your village has been very accepting of my racial difference." I could tell he was drunk. He walked quickly, but still swayed, and I wish I could say he walked in a straight line.

"Ha!" I laughed obnoxiously, slightly drunk as well. "I promised you my cousin, that you would be accepted! Even though I didn't think it would take this short of a time."

Without another word, we walked each other home, his guest housing right beside my house. I awoke that morning, sore headed, but not dreary. I walked over to my little hearth, its hot ashes still radiating heat. I grabbed a couple pieces of kindling and some straw. The fire started, I walked to the clay oven and started it as well, mostly burning straw, but some wood for a longer burn. I grabbed the kettle and filled it with water as well, leaving it to heat up. As soon as it started to boil I poured some into my cup and put the pewter tea dipper into it. I let it cool for a couple minutes and began meditating in the mean time.

Then suddenly I heard a knock on my door quiet, but progressively louder.

"Come in." I sighed. It was our head doctor and he was pacing his foot, nervously. "What is it Ishi?"

"Well Rayal, it seems that Rinku has a bad case of alcohol poisoning from drinking so much last night."

"Ugh, what am I supposed to do?" I asked gripping my hands together, getting agitated this early in the morning. Without another word I walked out of my house, my own head beginning to throb. I walked over to the guest housing and looked into it. Apparently Rinku had been moved to the hospital.

I got to the hospital soon after. It was strangely quiet. I looked around, saw one room with the lights on, and walked in.

"Rinku!" I shouted "Why are you up and about? You should be resting."

"Well... I think it was just a hangover, because I feel fine now."

I stomped out of the room, and slowly closed the door behind me, then stomped out of the hospital and back home.

"Argh!" I yelled out into the barren street.

* * *

The next day as the cleaning service cleaned the feast ground, I arranged a small tour of the defenses. We were to draft a new wall and resources were to be collected immediately. It was estimated that three quarters of the resources needed were to be harvested. It horrified me that our village only had a tiny amount of resources.

"Well Rinku, shall we be off?" I asked eagerly, rubbing my gloved hands, and rotating my shoulders.

"Well, I don't see why not. Let us be off!"

The time blasted away without any time at all. Actually, I barely do remember most of the events that had happened.

The day went by uneventfully and our progress was great. We were making it around the village in only half a day. But consequently, as I was arriving to the sparring grounds, I was informed that help was needed in the construction of the southern wall. I told the man that I would be there in quarter of an hour. As he started his horse in a canter, I was approaching the dojo where I was going to review the new and improved soldiers.

It was uneventful; the records said that on average the new recruit could spar with an instructor for four minutes better than the most primitive warriors fighting at less than fifteen seconds. Everyone had been promoted to an intermediate level, which was in my opinion great for a two day stretch, though not the best I have ever seen.

From here everything is a little blurry, due to some different altercations; I only remember little bits of hear-say. I was cantering easily towards the southern wall, where construction had already started. When I got there, I was ready to work; my energy was growing by the minute. I strapped a harness on and they pulled me up onto the structure. I got up there and took off my harness. Someone handed me a board, then the worst happened.

There I was, everything moving slow motion, the man in front of me turned with his board, someone shouted at him from the bottom, it hit me on the shoulder, and I lost my balance, next thing I knew, I was falling, the ground approaching quickly.

The last thing I remember was a loud thud, and some cracks.

Hayley:

The Memory Forager is a 250,000 word verse novel. Marci Ramirez is a carefree woman, mother of an adopted boy, whose life falls apart when her memories are lost as she becomes the new incarnation of a memory-eating beast.

The Memory Forager

A birch forest tinted blue
        by the early morning's breath. The sky is stark
and bright,
              but the scene is dull.
The branches above me claw at the
              eggshell blue sky
and my exhale mixes with the freezing air as a mist.
For once I feel like I blend in with my scene.
I don't like it.
        A coyote calls in the distance and
              my heart leaps into my chest.
        This is different, I declare. This
is new. Is this mine?
            I feel a tug at my chest.
No –
        in my chest. It aches,
              then it stings. It's pulling me forth and I
uncertainly let it.

Later, I find myself in a harbor.
        The feeling in my chest is now
burning a hole through my ribs. It sends shivers of pain down
              my nerves.

Compared to the numbness that usually
      seeps through my skin, I don't mind it.
I let the feeling spreading through my chest pull my feet.
      Step after step, my sore feet
carry me, stiffly, to a large cargo ship.
      Hesitation stops my body short of boarding the ship. The
sun made
its descent long ago. Stars scattered across the sky and
          lamps dotting the nearby street light my path.
I wait a moment before
      I continue. I carefully pull myself onto the ship
that rocks gently on the water.
      Not a sound lifts to the air,
          save for the creaking floorboards and
              the splash of waves against the hull.
My steps are cautious now,
      no longer sure of themselves as they followed
      the strong burning confined within
my ribs. I trail my grey fingers over a
      rope as I pass it. The stiff fibers prick the
surface of my skin and embed themselves in.
I feel roses of blood leaking carefully out of the injures,
      but I dismiss them while I walk.
Now directing my feet on my own,
        I move myself to the other end
      of the deck, and follow along the side.

The salty air stings my lungs and the gently burning
               embers in my chest. Soot trails behind me as my
bare feet step
      delicately
             along the floor. I can't help but pause as
    my cold toes meet with
a metal hatch.
    I kneel next to it, and slowly move to fiddle with the latch.
It gives way
             and I lift it with shaky, stiff fingers. As I stand
again,
     soot and ash fall around me like snow. I can feel the blood
pushing along,
             thick and lazy in my veins. I descend the stairs
    and find the space below to be
             comfortably warmer. Lanterns line the walls
                    and burn indefinitely. They flicker, but never
    die
             out.
    I wander through the room, finding crates
stacked precariously throughout.
The room is thick
     with dust. I'm eerily reminded of the
absence of rats.
Some crates lay open, broken with splinters strewn about.
     I peer in and find

nothing.

As I near the other end of the room, the embers in my chest alight.

    They glow and begin to heat up with a fury directing me to move.

There's a metal door,

    tarnished with age,

        waiting to be opened and given life

            again.

As I reach out, the burning downgrades

        into a dull ache.

    Something isn't right.

I try the doorknob and it doesn't budge.

        The door is locked.

I spin on my cold heel to go back up to the deck,

    but during the motion my head clouds with dizziness.

I squeeze my eyes shut

    and wait for it

        to fade

            away.

    When I open my eyes again,

        I'm not where I was.

    The ship is gone,

        replaced now by an empty ballroom.

    The dome ceiling is supported by golden pillars built against the walls.

        The change of scenery fills me

                                        with warmth.
I take a few steps further into the room and a tune sparks up,
        igniting the coals in my chest.
I spin on my toes,
               as an old swing song
      plays across my ears.
The patterned floor scuffed by years of shoes
        is a welcome change to the frozen ship deck.
The record skips, and I pause.
        As it picks up again, it's distorted.
I strain my ears to make out the upbeat tune I had heard
               once before.
        The singer's voice reaches my ears in clips of song,
             but the beat is misshapen and unrecognizable.
I don't move, save for glancing down at my grey feet.
They look as lifeless as always and the
        ashes dancing down to the floor at the movement
             seem sickeningly familiar
                 as they scatter around my toes.
The scenario is gut wrenching and a feeling that I cannot place
        turns to an ache rising from my gut to my heart.
               I feel sick.
I bring my gaze up again and listen to the out-of-place,
    horribly distorted song. The ache fades away,
    leaving me feeling hollow.
              I can't help but wonder if it was just a feeling,

or if the coals in my chest are burning away at the rest of me.

I inhale, and realize that I wouldn't care if they did.

Do I even need my organs?

I can't answer that.

I turn to look at the rest of the ballroom in this new light.

The first thing I realize is that

there are no doors.

I look down at the lowly burning coals

I tap them, and feel my finger sting.

"Where to now?" I speak out loud. My voice is rough from lack of use.

The coals flash orange and white,

burning with fervor.

I close my eyes and listen closely.

The feeling in my chest whispers,

warmly, lowly.

We are going somewhere new.

My head swims with dizziness once again.

My stomach lurches and I stumble on my feet.

I feel dirt against my foot as it hits the ground.

This is new. I swallow and collect my wits about me.

I open my eyes and stand up

straight.

Dust swims through the air,

catching the dim yellow lights.

  I'm surrounded
by large shelves of crates.
    The ceiling is tall and full of rafters.
  This is a warehouse.
  My ears catch a repetitive noise, coming from farther in the
building.
"Do I follow it?"
  Do as you wish.
I hum, finding the voice of the burning calming.
It's delicate and
   ethereal.
    I stretch and my back cracks.
  My feet move smoothly now, but I walk
    on the tips of my toes. The dust and dirt
  strewn across the floor
    tickle my feet as they move.
The shelves pass me by.
   Some crates have lids astray and others
     are busted open.
My legs carry me to the middle of the warehouse as if I know the
route by heart.
  Maybe –
  maybe I do.
I notice bits of tin and iron
    scattered across the floor. The light becomes
     brighter and more organic the farther I go.

The burning in my torso flares. I stop.
      The scene before is magical –
          or… memorable.
The roof of the warehouse has caved in.
      It is being taken back by vines and young trees.
Weeds are bursting through the stone
            with vengeance in their energy.
Rubble is scattered around them, and the floor is
      overcome
            with moss.
"I know this."
I know. The sentence is punctuated by another soft sound.
      It's water,
dripping into a puddle in the middle of the scene.
      I take a deep breath of the clean air
          and feel it enter my skin.
          It's an amazing improvement from the dusty air
I was breathing before.
      "Is this all?"
No. Climb out.
    "Climb?" I asked.
The voice hummed in reply.
My feet began to move
          on their own.
I stepped into the middle of the cool puddle
      and felt a chill rise up

my spine.

I watched my toes stretch in the puddle
      and I dragged them along
            and the grime
     and ash
washed away.

The temperature of the water
      on my weathered feet was a welcome change.

I moved delicately towards the ruble stacked
nearby leading to the hole left by
         the caved in ceiling.

Sunlight warmed my back as I stopped
     and looked up at the sky.

The eggshell left behind by
     a newborn robin stretched above
my head with evergreen cracks
        splitting from the edges.

I could hear birds singing their wakeup calls
and knew this was the first time
       in a long while
    that I've heard that noise.

I didn't want to move.

I could feel the embers in my chest
           going cold
    and it bothered me
but I couldn't bring myself to move.

Then, something changed.

The coo of a dove hollowed my bones

                                        and lifted my feet.

I stepped out of the puddle

        and bent at the hip

                and began to ascend the caved in roof.

I hopped along like I weighed nothing at all

        and rose to the surface with ease.

The warehouse must have been

                partially underground

because my feet landed on dirt

                and grass.

The abandoned building

stood atop a large hill bordered by more,

                          smaller,

      rolling hills.

The scenery seemed to be agricultural lands because

the hills were covered in colorful fields dotted

        by the

                odd

        pine tree.

I took a breath of the

        clean air

                and straightened my shoulders.

The coals in my chest began

                to burn

again.

    I took a step and stumbled a little.

Dizziness flooded my head again and when it faded

                I knew I was somewhere new.

I lifted my head and almost forgot to straighten my back

        as I realized where I was.

It hit me immediately.

"You know where you are."

The ethereal voice returned and that

            wasn't a question.

I was standing in the middle of an art studio.

Sun is let into

        the glowing room through windows on one side

            and a door on the other.

Chipped and carved

        wooden tables with splattered paint and scattered pencils littering the tops.

The room has stacked stools and easels around the edges and it feels

              like

    home.

The one part that unsettles me is that

        the room is empty.

I'm the only one there.

"This is my old art classroom."

"Yes."

"Why am I here?" A shock of pain sparked as a piece of my torso began to burn.

 That was the only response I got.

"I know who I am." I said aloud. "I… Why do I know who I am?"

"You need to."

"Why?"

"You need to know to protect yourself." I braced myself on the nearest table and began

       to focus on my breathing.

Something clicked in my mind.

"These are all my old memories." The voice did not respond.

"Why are they empty?"

Again, I got no answer.

"Where do we go now?"

My mind clouded.

Next I found myself standing in the middle

       of a street.

The street lamps were lit up,

casting puddles of orange onto the cracked street.

The pavement was cool on my feet and I brushed some small rocks aside.

The wind was warm

and the sky was just beginning to deepen as the sun fell behind

       the mountains around.

The gentle wind was comforting.

What I wasn't prepared for, was seeing the first person I've seen
        in some time.

A door on the nearby house swung open and a child hopped out. He hurried across the deep green lawn
        and slowed as he approached me.

I offered a nervous smile
        and the child's wide eyes searched mine,
              and then fell to my hand
        as he reached out for it.

I hesitated then moved it closer
        for him to take.

The child took my hand in both and beamed.

I felt my chest burn hot and the hole felt like it was growing.

My torso was left in searing pain from the white hot coals
        alight

inside.

The child didn't seem to be worried whatsoever.

He cast a glance at the embers in my chest and then
        turned to look down the lonely road.

I felt my arm tugged gently by the child and he began to walk.

I followed him.

We walked the length of the road
        and continued
              on an adjacent street.

This street was darker as it was in the shadows of trees.

The kid would look back at me every now and then
        as if he wasn't sure if I was actually there,
following,
              despite holding my hand.
I mainly kept my eyes high, watching the color of the sky change
        along with the scenery
as we kept on walking.
 Maybe I should try talking to him?
"What's your name?" I offered.
The child looked back at me with a confused frown.
"You don't remember?"
 I scrunched my face up and wracked my brain.
After some moments, I sighed.
"No."
This time, the boy didn't look back and didn't seem to mind.
He just kept on walking
      down
          the street.
            I resolved to listen to the tapping of his shoes
     and the muffled shuffling sounds
of my bare feet on the pavement.
We went on like that for a while.
The sun had fallen and the night air was warm.
I found the quiet town soothing, if
     a little creepy.
I was grateful for the warm pools of light splattered over the road,

       along with the cool light provided
            by the white moon and stars.
Deep blue,
bordering on indigo,
shaded by the cold stars was a perfect backdrop for this scene. The child tugged my arm again and stopped.
He had his eyes scrunched by the friendly grin on his face.
"We're here?" I asked.
"Where is here?" I stretched my shoulders and looked around.
"We're at the park!" The child chirped.
Sure enough, I had been led to a playground.
"Oh," I offered
      a smile,
           "do you want to swing?"
The kid nodded and began to hurry off to the swing set.
"Do you want me to push you?"
"No! You swing too!" The kid called as he twisted and sat down on the swing,
            but waited there for me.
I was walking along the rocks carefully
    to keep from hurting my feet anymore
        and the child seemed patient enough.
I was also having some trouble breathing
as the burning coals in my chest seemed to be growing hotter once again.
    Once I made it over to the swing set and sat down,

the kid was still watching me and waiting for me to move.
Only after I began to swing did he move.
He followed my lead now, swinging just as high as I was.
      The cool air rushing past my face was refreshing.
To see the stars rushing
          a little bit closer
     each time I swung up
urged me to let go and reach for them
and for a moment, I almost did.
It only took a moment,
     a fraction of time where the electricity in the air buzzed
          close to my heart
     and I knew something was off.
Only a moment, and I was
                          falling.
I feel like any tangible ground I had before had been
     ripped
          away as I was pulled
right out of reality.
     Before I could have a chance to get a grip on where I was however,
                it was gone.
I was shoved back to the ground and hit it roughly.
I was on dry, rocky dirt
     and I knew
before I even moved

that I would be cut up from it.
I pushed myself up and looked around.
My gut went cold as I recognized the scene.
It sent a chill
    through
        my
            bones
and I immediately felt the heat in my chest
              ignite.
"No... This-" I struggled to find my words,
"I didn't do this!"
I searched desperately for something,
    someone else
        for comfort.
I was sitting on the ground in the midst of
    mindless,
        standing corpses
as I felt like I was
    pulling
            myself apart
    at
      the
seams.
I called out,
    and no one came.
I took in a shuddering breath and lifted myself to my feet.

I felt incredibly heavy and

            unbalanced

as I began to weave between the people standing, staring blankly. I tried not to look at their faces.

      I knew they didn't look tortured,

    maybe just surprised,

 but I didn't want to see.

My heart was hammering against my blackened ribcage

        but it sounded weak

   compared to my crackling skin.

I stumbled as I picked up the pace.

    I didn't know where I was going

        but I knew I had to hurry.

My vision was bleary with tears and I could feel my feet

  warm with blood

  but I kept going.

The world was spinning around my distraught mind and I felt

  I would collapse at a moment's notice.

Once again a moment

    was all

     it

  took.

A moment, and everything stopped.

    I was facing something a little larger than me.

I was alarmed by the change in surroundings

   but soon realized it was just a mirror.

A single,

clean object

      in this mess of swallowed minds and cracked rock.

I knew what I was being asked to do.

I took another deep breath and my legs moved for me.

    One,

        two,

           three steps

before I was right in front of my reflection.

I raised my eyes slowly.

Standing before me was something terrifically animalistic.

The patchy black hair and pink, raw skin didn't match mine at all.

It had marred ears and fat, yellow teeth with globs of drool falling around them.

In time with my own breaths, the beast's back and chest

rose

           and fell.

    I felt

        sick.

I felt like I was someone entirely different.

    Rather, I felt like no one at all.

My heart leapt into my throat as I met the thing's eyes.

It's startling, brilliant teal eyes.

I lifted a hand to reach forth

        and my touch met the cold surface of the mirror.

On the other side, a broken, clawed paw reached
                              for me.
My world crumbled at my feet.

       I am the memory forager.
My duty is to consume memories until a mind is rendered useless.
                I am an entity reinventing itself
as the tides of the universe change and pull me to and fro.
       In my past, my hunger was ravenous.
I totaled the world's population within hours.
       I... am not like that
                      anymore.

I sunk to the ground in front of my reflection.
"Do you understand?"
An otherworldly voice pushed through my thoughts.
I took a few shallow breaths before licking my lips and answering.
"I don't want to."
The voice didn't come back.
I distantly wondered if I upset it.
The forefront of my mind was focused on what I was experiencing.
I looked up at my reflection again and gazed into its tired eyes.
If this is me... whose memories were the ones I saw before?
        Who danced freely in ballrooms
              and hitched rides on cargo ships?
                    I didn't have that kind of freedom.

At the moment
> I couldn't understand much but that,
>> at least,
> I knew.

My chest ached.
I raised a hand to feel the expanding hole and
> when I pulled away with a burnt finger,
>> I saw
> it was darkened
with ash.
My gaze once again lifted to the mirror
and I found myself fixed on the beast's mangled chest.
It, too, had embers burning in its torso.
It's uneven ribs were smoking
> idly
> as the red embers continued to burn.

"This really is me..."
> I murmured to myself.

Who was I looking at before?
Something clicked into place.
Was I even looking at memories before?
> Everything was empty.

I was alone in the forest,
> alone on the ship,
>> in the ballroom,

>   the warehouse,
>
>   and the art class.
>
> At the playground, only
>
>   a child
>
>   was with me.
>
> I took in a shaky breath and curled in on myself.
>
> I felt so lost,
>
>   so...
>
>   alien.
>
> I had no one to consult,
>
>   no one
>
>   to ask
>
> for comfort.
>
> Not even a teardrop would fall from my aching eyes.
>
> My heart was still hammering on against my burning ribs.
>
> That was a comfort
>
>   at least.
>
> No matter how much I felt like I was falling apart,
>
>   my heart was still beating
>
>   for me.
>
> I took another deep breath, this one finally steady.
>
> I pushed myself back up onto my feet and rubbed my eyes.
>
> "Where to now?" I called out to the voice that's been accompanying me.
>
> I didn't get an answer.
>
> Instead, the familiar dizziness came over my mind.

The dark scenery changed to a sunny, warm green.

I was at the edge of a stream, standing beside a willow tree
              with a swing
    hanging
from a branch.

The sunlight warmed my skin.

Such a welcoming scene nearly brought me to tears again.

My mind was flooded with thoughts

as I tried to decipher what was going on.

Why was this happening to me?

Why was I being tortured like this?

"You need to do your job." The voice chimed in.

I couldn't help a stressed whine from rising from my throat.

"I've done my job!" I snapped back.

Distantly in the air I heard the sound of chimes come and go.

I let myself fall to my knees in the dirt.

The earth here was soft and cradling compared

to the rocky ground I was on before.

                  I didn't find it any more comforting.

I sat back and pulled my legs up to chest,
          watching the water in the stream
      play along the rocks by the bank.

After some silence, I spoke up.

"Have I been here before?"

"Yes." The voice answered immediately.

"What about the other places?"

I got a confirming noise in response.

At least satisfied with that, I sighed and sunk
                          in on myself.

I don't know how long I was there

but it was some time before anything really changed.

The sun had fallen behind the trees and left me in a red glow
      when the voice
            returned.

"Would you like to go now?"

It asked.

I didn't answer right away.

"I'd like to know what's going on." I countered   quietly.

All the voice said
        was a simple
          "you'll
            find
               out."

"I'm so lost."

I explained in a pained voice,
    as if whoever was out there couldn't see me.

I'm sure they could
     and they must know how confused I am.

I let out a shaky sigh when I didn't get an answer
      and I lowered my head onto my knees.

It wasn't much longer until my mind clouded
     and I

                was somewhere new.

The room was glowing,
        even if it was dusty
    and dirty.
The tanks weren't grimy with algae
and all the fish were still swimming around.
I unfolded my legs and looked around in awe.
I'm in an aquarium...
All of the large tanks around me towered over my small figure.
There were lots of small fish
      but the large ones were what caught my attention.
They're so beautiful...
I pushed myself up onto my feet and moved to the closest tank to look.
I gently spread my palm onto the cool glass
 and gazed into the blue water above.
The building was filled with
      whirring
          and
              buzzing
from what must be filters and lights,
    along with the odd bubbling sounds.
I found myself dearly hoping
I could just experience this - that there was nothing
                    that would change;

                no clues for me to discover.
And for now, there wasn't.
  The environment was soothing.
Everything was muted and slow.
Even the coals in my chest had relaxed their job of eating away at my torso.
I turned and began to move around the room,
  smiling at the fish that were curious enough to swim closer
                      to the glass of their tanks
          to gaze back at me.
I almost laughed when I realized
my grey-blue tones must be blending in well with the blue-green light
        casting onto the metal floors and walls.
 My body began to feel light once again.
Of course, nothing good can last.
  The cracking sound
                reverberated
        in my
    bones.
It sends a chill throughout my body
      that ignites the flame
              eating me alive.
I stumble back blindly as the pain
    shakes
        my limbs.

Next, I can't breathe.
The crashing sound of water spilling into the room
      fills my senses.
White and blue pull me back
and my head crashes against the nearest tank.

      I black out.

I'm itchy.
The first thing I notice when I wake up
      is that
            my skin is crawling and warm.
I don't want to open my eyes but the itching is
                incessant.
Opening my eyes brings me to realize
      that my skin is covered
with ants.
I roll and leap to my feet,
      staggering but persisting.
I brush the ants away as best as I can,
          stumbling through the sand.
Straightening my back, I look around and take in my surroundings.
      The white sand rolls in front of me,
crystalline waves washing against the beach.
The scene was nice, but my head was still spinning from before.
I passed a hand over my face and rubbed my eyes

to clear my vision.

The sky was bright, the colour nearly matching my eyes.

I blinked a couple times at the bright sun.

Sand was stretching as far as I could see

                              but

        no matter how much I moved or strained my eyes

to catch sight of another person,

                not a single other figure met my eyes.

I sighed and stretched my back.

I felt like something was pushing right at the front of my mind, ready to show itself but I

                      couldn't reach it.

Was this another memory?

It must be, there isn't another person in sight.

Certainly there can't be something here that I have to look for, it's all beach.

        I curled my toes into the sand as I thought,

                then sat back down.

The warmth of the sun-baked sand on my skin was comforting.

        Why am I even here?

The voice said I'm here to protect myself but...

            I feel like I'm being

    torn   *apart.*

They also said that I've been to all these places before.

            Have I been here?

I turned my head to look out into the teal water

                fighting against the baby blue sky.
Along with the rushing waves, I could also hear gulls calling out in the distance.
        Regardless, I couldn't see them.
I let out a sigh.
        Looking down at myself now,
I noticed ashes spilling out onto my clothes.
        My pants were torn along my legs,
                speckled with dirt and mud.
Even my shirt looked weathered and worn.
        I often didn't wear shoes
                and could certainly feel the consequences now.
My feet were crusted with dry blood,
                        mud,
                            dirt,
        and soot.
The heat from the sand was soothing the pain in them.
I laid back to allow the warmth to work
on my stiff back and shoulders as well.
The sounds of the beach lulled me into a more relaxed state
but I didn't let myself fall asleep.
I kept my eyes open and trained on the cloud-streaked sky above.
I wanted to stay there and allow time to pass around me
but after some time without the sky changing at all,
                        I became restless.
I sat up with a grumble and began to look around.

    Everything was still the same.

I got to my feet.

      I called out to whoever has been guiding me.

"What am I doing here?"

"Do you remember this place?" The voice asked gently.

I let my shoulders
          fall.

"No." After a moment of quiet, I added,
     "I don't."

I heard a familiar chiming of bells and hesitated to move.

Within a moment, the beach was now bordered by all sorts of tropical trees and plants and I could see the birds that I had heard the whole time.

The ocean's horizon was interrupted by cliffs on the sides and rocks breaking the surface out in the water.

I almost gasped at the beauty of the sight but the same
  tick,
     pushing at my mind,
         came back.

I frowned.

Have I ever been to a tropical beach?

I took a breath of the salty air
       and moved closer to the tree line.

The warm green leaves in my sight are a welcome change.

  I let a smile split my face.

  The voice returned.

"Have you been here before?"

I took a moment to dwell on the question.

This place seemed

                        familiar.

"I believe I have."

  I answered, now furrowing my brow in thought.

"What do you remember?"

      I closed my eyes gently.

The warmth of the sun spread through my being

      and

              I

                      relaxed.

 Taking a moment to breathe,

I opened my mouth.

"I remember searching

                    for seashells

        when I still lived alone.

Every day I went,

I would find one that was still being used by a little critter.

 Once I adopted my son we would come

and search for the smaller beachgoers on purpose.

I wanted him to observe life passively; without disrupting it.

It didn't take him long to realize

that he wasn't supposed to touch the creatures, but watch them

from a distance.

We never ran into another person on this beach.

It was our peaceful little sanctuary."

The air filled with chimes, as if the voice was humming.

"Who was your son?" It asked.

  I opened my eyes again.

The sky was overcast now and the beach looked much darker.

           I frowned.

Some moments later, I answered.

"I don't know."

My mind clouded.

Jessie:

Secrets of a Songbird is an incomplete 150,000 word young adult novel set in 1940's San Francisco. Ryan is an aspiring jazz musician. Brendon is a cabaret dancer. When they cross paths, neither one of them expects the serenely tragic nightmare that will transcend time and history.

WARNING: graphic language & content.

Secrets of a Songbird

Chapter II
March 7th, 1943
The Rose's Thorn – San Francisco, California

BRENDON

When Brendon pictured living on his own, it sure as hell didn't include seemingly endless days spent draped in satin and lace or coated with French perfume. It had, however, included an apartment of his own, with freshly painted walls and a nice couch. Maybe he'd have gotten a dog, or something. Maybe a bird. Truthfully, anything could have been better than living in a cement box.

Calling this place a home was a stretch. When you think of home, what do you think of? Maybe you call to mind images of a house with a fence or a mother tightly wound into a striped apron, baking in the kitchen. A place where the only satin that existed was upon the soft petals of the flowers in the beds that lined the front of the house. Home looked like a street where you used to play hockey with sticks crafted by your father. At the very least, home had a warm bed, not some dingy second or third hand couch. Brendon could think of all of the things that a home looked like. Visualizing the opposite was not something of a laborious task, and this was because it was every day that he would float past the bar and the stage, down a dingy hallway where a singular light flickered at the ceiling and he would find 'home'. Home was a cold room in the basement of a cabaret. Home was a vanity dotted with bulbs and lined with makeup palettes and ornate bottles of perfume. Home was a worn leather couch that stank of mildew. Home was devoid of any life aside from the pained dancer who spent cold nights curled upon the couch.

 Brendon had been given the night off after two long weeks of working the stage. He'd been made up like a painted doll, and wondered as he peered into the mirror if he would ever be able to remove the rosy hue left behind by the blush on his cheeks. His jacket pulled tight over his shoulders, his elbow propped up on the top of the vanity. He cupped his chin. His eyes narrowed as he peered at his reflection in the convexed glass vase of fresh lilies left as a gift by a man in the bar. His gaze danced along his slightly distorted features; his full, pouted lips, his deep amber eyes. The cheekbones that seemed almost razor sharp, and the prominent jaw devoid of any stubble. Smooth—just as the customers liked him.

 A tall, slender figure appeared behind him in the dimmed light. Brendon's gaze shifted, and he caught sight of a navy suit-jacket, a black fedora clutched to a broad chest. He didn't need to shift his eyes upward to be able to know who had approached him.

 "Hey, Dall," Brendon greeted, his eyes dropping to the vanity before him. His gaze found a pear shaped bottle of perfume and he reached forward to grasp it between his fingers. He smoothed his fingertips over the ridges implanted into the glass. He picked at the label with his thumb absently as he felt a hand lay gently on his shoulder. His eyes flicked quickly to the left and caught sight of Dallon's rings, the large golden ones he'd said had been passed down to him from his father. Brendon pressed his cheek to the top of that hand.

"Hey, sugar." Dallon greeted with a gentle smile. Brendon felt his skin prickle. "Where've you been?"

Brendon's eyes moved back down to the vanity, where he watched his own fingers flex, examining his knuckles and what they might've looked like if he were fortunate enough to have golden rings planted proudly upon each of them. "I went boozin' down at Sam's.'S my night off. I deserved it." He swivelled in his seat, minding the creak the old wood gave beneath his weight. When he settled, he looked up and captured Dallon's piercing blue gaze. His stomach lurched.

"Sure did." Dallon replied with a grin. He swiped his tongue over his teeth, then clicked his tongue and set his fedora on the vanity. *Brendon's* vanity. The younger boy scowled at the action briefly, but turned his attention elsewhere. He knew better than to rag on Dallon.

"Where were you?" Brendon inquired.

Dallon chewed on his lip. Brendon watched how Dallon's mouth twisted while he nibbled on the thin skin. He wondered why he did it—whether it was by nerves, or if he enjoyed the metallic taste of blood oozing on his tongue when he bit a little too hard.

"I's finishin' my shift upstairs. You talked to Shane yet today?"

Brendon shook his head. *Thank God*, he thought. *Every day I don't have to consort with a snake like him is a blessing.* "Nah. Why? 'S he cuttin' my hours or somethin'?"

Dallon scoffed, then turned to spit into the trash bin set aside the vanity. "*Cuttin'* them?" He asked incredulously. "Honey, he's uppin' them if an'thing." He dipped his hand into his pocket to fish out a pack of Camels. He popped the flap of cardboard and pulled one from the row nearest the front of the package and tossed it into his mouth, as if it were a kernel of popped corn. He brought his palm up and cupped the flame from the match, shaking it away once the end of the white stick burned orange. Brendon watched with narrowed eyes. It was something he'd seen Dallon do before countless times. He had memorized such moments in their history together.

He would lie down on the couch; nude body wrapped loosely in a crisp, white sheet and watch the older man toss his smoke into his mouth while hunched over on the discoloured rug, back pressed against the couch.

He'd seen him do it as he slipped back into his crisp white shirt and fancy suit jacket.

He'd watched him do it as he left—he always left.

Watching Dallon smoke had become something methodic. Routine. He'd spit, then pull the pack from the folds of either denim or polyester, toss it in the air, deftly grab it between his lips before it had a chance to fall. Brendon realized now, as he watched him do it for the thousandth time, that he hated it. Not because he couldn't stand the smell of tobacco, but because when Dallon smoked it only meant that he was stressed.

And that meant that Brendon ended up with the brunt of it.

Brendon's dark eyes widened. Dallon merely flicked his gaze up to the poster hung on the wall—an advert for the cabaret that had been posted around the city in the club's earliest years. He brought the cigarette to his lips and sucked, his exhale being the only sound that untucked the blanket of silence that had fallen over them. Brendon winced.

"You's jokin'." Brendon denied, pushing his fingers through his dark hair. He had to be joking. His blood had run cold.

Dallon flicked the ash off of the end of his cigarette. Brendon watched it flitter through the air until it fell to the floor, narrowly missing the edge of the trashcan. Dallon shook his head. "Nah. He's talkin' about 'business opportunities' and whatnot. I say the guy's a loon. He's sure got his mind made, though." He explained, extending his hand to flick the ash into the ashtray properly this time.

"What the hell do you mean by *'business opportunities'*, Dall? C'mon, don' be pansyin' around this. Give it to me straight."

Dallon's head turned, eyes widening at the sudden boldness.

Brendon sank back into the chair some. It was rare that he talked back like that. He had learned to keep his jaw wired shut after a series of unfortunate altercations in which he'd ended up with a bruised cheek and a loosened tooth.

"He's askin' you dancers t'start sleepin' with the customers."

Brendon didn't register the words at first. For the beginning few moments of the silence between them, Brendon didn't move. He didn't blink, breathe, or even *think* in those moments. When the weight of those words finally began to seep into his bones, into his shaky stream of consciousness, he felt his hands begin to tremble. His throat was tightening and curiously, his eyes were stinging with impending tears. "No," he breathed.

"Yeah. Tol' me this evenin'." Dallon said evenly. Sucking on the smoke one last time, he flicked the ash away and tossed the butt into the trash. He lifted a hand and placed it where it'd been before upon Brendon's shoulder. "Don' worry about it, tootse—"

"Don't touch me."

Dallon's eyes widened.

"Wha's your problem, sugar? C'mon, don't be like this." Dallon cooed, dropping his hand. He waited a moment, then reached out to touch him once again.

Brendon had seen this all before, of course. That was the thing about Dallon Weekes—he was a sweetheart on the surface, but pure malevolence beneath the facade. He was the type of man that could manipulate you into doing whatever he wanted you to do with a simple suave smile, a gentle gaze.

Brendon scooted back, perhaps a little too violent, and felt his back crack when it collided with the wooden edge of the vanity. A few bottles toppled over and clattered against one another.

Dallon's shoulders rose, his nostrils flared.

"I said *don't* touch me—" Brendon snarled, but was soon cut off by the sobering sting of a hand slapping the softness of his cheek. For a split second, Brendon's mind was blank, vision blurred. His eyes slowly opened, the fuzzy carpet coming back into his line of vision. He felt wetness on his upper lip. *Was that a tear? God, don't let that be a tear. Do* not *show him weakness.*

Brendon's knuckles were white as they gripped the chair to keep himself from falling to the floor. It wasn't easy, however. He felt hazy, and addled with pain. His vision had cleared, and he watched a single crimson droplet fall from his face, spattering on the cement. With the sight of blood, Brendon felt something boiling inside him. Something rebellious and dangerous. This was the last time.

He stood, the chair shooting forward and knocking into Dallon's pelvis.

The man keeled over, only briefly before his head snapped up, eyes wild. *Fearsome.* He grabbed the chair's back, throwing it aside with a single arm. Brendon heard the wood splinter when it hit the wall, but he didn't look. His eyes were focused solely on Dallon.

Dallon lunged for him, but Brendon skittered to the side. The elder man grabbed at suddenly empty air. When Dallon's meaty hands met with the vanity, a few bottles rolled to the edge and fell to the floor, shattering. The sound of broken glass crunched beneath Dallon's boot as he turned on Brendon once again.

He tried to dash away once more, but this time, his feet could not carry him as fast as he willed them to and Dallon's hand thrust out and gripped his bicep roughly. Brendon winced as fingertips dug viciously into the muscle. "Who d'you think you is, hmm? Talkin' t'me like you's the Queen of fuckin' Sheba." Dallon hissed as he jerked Brendon's arm, bringing him closer. Brendon's heart was in his throat, his skin burning with the knowledge that this just might be the night that that unruly mouth of his landed him in a big oak box. But knowing Shane and his stringiness with money, Brendon would be tied to a cinderblock and tossed over the Golden Gate.

"I ain't livin' with it no more, Dallon." Brendon yelped, trying to wrangle his arm free. Dallon yanked harder and shoved his slender frame, sending him into the wall. Brendon's head snapped backwards, and smacked the cement, but he didn't whine. *Be strong*, he told himself. *He won't do nothin'.*

"Ain't livin' with what?" Dallon snapped, his face close to Brendon's as he braced his forearm against his chest. Brendon's breath came in short, ragged gasps as panic set in. Still, his eyes remained steely with defiance.

"This," he hissed. "You ain't gonna lay a hand on me no more."

Dallon's lips twisted into an unsettling smirk. Brendon's skin was crawling. "And just what'cha gonna do out there in the big bad world without me, huh?"

"'M gonna live without bruises, that's for damn sure." Brendon barked, the waves of defiant anger burning through him like a raging fire. It coursed through his veins and set his heart ablaze. A satisfied smirk bloomed on his lips. "I'm leavin' this hole. 'N I'm sure as hell leavin' you too."

There was weight on his throat now. His windpipe tightened under pressure. Everything burned, but Dallon's hand felt like ice as it closed like a vise around Brendon's throat. Tighter. *Tighter*.

Brendon fought back instinctively. He clawed desperately at Dallon's hand but the older man's grip was unyielding. Dark spots dotted Brendon's vision, lips parted as he futilely attempted to fill his burning lungs. He was weakening.

Dallon forced Brendon's jaw upwards, forcing the younger's gaze to fix on the ceiling. Brendon had stared at this roof a thousand times while Dallon had his way with him in the sweaty evenings that followed his shift upstairs. But damn, did it ever look different with the red stars exploding over his eyes. With the possibility that it may be the last sight his eyes ever captured.

"You ungrateful tramp," Dallon hissed. He clamped harder onto Brendon's throat. Brendon suppressed a cough. He felt his cheeks burning red, his eyes bulging.. "You's nothin' without me. I gotcha this job when you's just a scrappy teenager. Now you wanna leave? Why? Because the big boss man wants you to spread your legs? You ain't never had an issue with doin' that before. You's nothin' but a money-whore. Ain't nobody outside these walls that'll hire your ass. I'll make sure of that. But I don't gotta worry much 'bout you leavin', do I? Cause you know, Brendon. You know that if you do, I'll find ya. Think you's a sneaky little runt? I got eyes in this city. Believe me, boy, I'll find ya. And when I do? Boy, you *better* be fuckin' scared."

Brendon's throat was raw when he sucked in a breath, collapsing to the ground. Immediately, he was coughing, gasping for air. The floor was cool against his skin, and he found solace in the sensation of the cement, of the rough surface of the rug beneath his fingertips. His fingers splayed out, touching everything, memorizing sensations. He had been so close, so close.

He looked up, eyes red and watered. He didn't dare speak. His eyes moved down, and caught sight of Dallon's foot, extended backwards. He squeezed his eyes shut, bracing for impact, fists winding around the frayed edges of the rug.

"Weekes!" A familiar voice bellowed from beyond Dallon. Brendon's eyes snapped open to the bartender—Andrew. Andrew, or Andy as he was known by most everyone in the club was a beefed up man with tattoos that lined each of his arms, both of his legs and much of his torso. Thank God he showed up, because everyone, even Dallon the *bouncer* was afraid of Andy. "How many times do you gotta be told?" Andy barked, closing in on Dallon. Dallon's foot lowered and in several strides, Andy's fist was clenched around the collar of Dallon's shirt, and dragged him away from Brendon's collapsed frame, shoving him into the wall beside him.

"Whoa, man, take it easy—" Dallon spluttered, his fingers gripping Andy's thick wrist in an attempt to push him off.

Andy's eyes narrowed. "Take it easy? I walk in on you beatin' the living hell out of Brendon, and you expect me to take it *easy*? If I ever see you lay a hand on him again, I *swear*, Dallon, I will castrate you with my bare hands."

Brendon heaved for breath on the floor and rolled onto his back, his eyes finally closing. The cool cement felt indescribable on his aching shoulders. He could hear some shuffling, a little grunting. Then, a body hit the floor with a reverberating thud. "Get your scrawny ass out of here, Weekes." Andy barked.

When Brendon was finally able to muster the strength to roll his head to the side and open his eyes, he watched Dallon pick himself up off the floor and gather his things.

Brendon's chest heaved with a sigh of relief when Dallon left. He hadn't registered it until then, but Andy had picked him up off the floor and carried him to the couch. His breath stuttered as he drew in another unstable breath. His lungs still burned.

"Why is it always me?"

Andy was hunched over as he swept the broken glass from the broken perfume bottle onto a sheet of paper to dispose of. There was silence between them for a moment.

"I dunno, Bren. I don't," Andy finally said. "but sooner or later, he'll learn. Don't know when, Don' know how."

As Brendon extended his legs and eased himself out, he looked up at his friend. Despite himself, he managed a smile. Andy cocked an eyebrow and motioned to the space on the couch unoccupied by Brendon's legs. Brendon gave a short nod and shifted. Tears burned on the brims of his eyelids. "What's wrong with me?" Brendon asked, averting his gaze. He looked back to his hands folded in his lap and shut his eyes, a single tear rolling over the swell of his cheek.

"Bren," Andy cooed. He planted a comforting hand on Brendon's ankle. Brendon felt his calloused fingertips massage gentle circles into the skin. "There ain't nothin' wrong with you."

"Then why does he do this?" Brendon sobbed.

"I can't—"

"I ain't his property. He's been treatin' me like this for years, Andy. I can't do it no more."

Andy remained silent.

Brandon:

Skate Dreams is a forty-five hundred word action drama novella. After witnessing his brother's death, a street skater living in Kelowna is trying to make his dreams a reality.

Skate Dreams

THERE ARE THIRTEEN MILLION SKATEBOARDERS IN NORTH AMERICA ALONE. TEN MILLION IDENTIFY THEMSELVES AS STREET SKATERBOARDERS. THIS IS THEIR STORY.

My legs grew heavy as I approached the staircase. Right before the first step down I popped a 360 flip and flew past all five steps and rolled away. All of the skaters in the area came to a standing elevation and gave me applause. "Go, go, go cops!" All the skaters froze and started to clear out.

I immediately grabbed my bag and followed my friends to a fence that was roughly seven feet tall. As I looked behind me I could see skaters being shoved to the ground and being read their rights. When we got to the fence we all threw our skateboards over the top and started to mount the fence but not even half way up a cop got a hold of my bag and started to wrench me down. With only one choice I slid my arm through the straps and jumped over the fence, crossed the street and disappeared behind a semi going by.

Later we all met up at the lobby that had a nice patch of grass to rest on.

"Yo, did you see how many cops there were? That was ridiculous." Mikey panted. We all called him Mikey because he had bright orange hair that covered his eyes like Michelangelo of the kid show *Teenage Mutant Ninja Turtles*, not to add all the freckles he had, too. As I rolled up to the group from being far behind the group all my friends glanced at me, "I thought you got popped homie, where you were?" Joey asked.

"I fell a bit behind but security got my bag, man." I muttered in a low tone while sitting down on the patch of grass.

"Screw your bag! You could've been on your way to jail right now!" Rob chimed in. Rob used to be my inspiration until he made it clear that he had to be better than anyone, no matter what.

"Well we can't just stand here lets go skate at the grocery store." I suggested.

"Hell no. That place is littered with cops setting up cameras." Ryan added while lighting a cigarette. I grabbed my board and let them know that we could go to the Woodley ledge where cops weren't allowed. The group agreed and hopped on our boards and headed out.

"Slow down, I'm a smoker," Ryan added again while he was doing a slow jog struggling to keep up.

As we rolled by the spot at the grocery store there was a skater being beaten by at least six security guards.

"Crazy, flip a board and grind a few ledges and people lose their mind." Ryan said as he gestured towards the store that we used to skate at.

We then finally arrived to the ledge and of course Rob had to hit it first. His first grind was a kick flip crook that he bailed at the end.

"You got to be kidding me, man," he muttered as he walked back to the start.

"If you keep centered on your front truck you're in for it," I tried suggesting.

"Did I ask you for advice? Matter of fact, let's see you do it," he snapped back, pointing at the ledge.

I didn't hesitate. I hopped on my board and rolled up to the ledge staying centered so I wouldn't make the same mistake. I slid the whole thing and rolled away. As I went to look at Rob, I ran into a mid-30s man with dark brown hair.

"Can't you see the sign? No skating allowed! I don't want to get charged when one of you breaks your neck!" he scolded.

"It's a ledge. Nobody's going to break anything except for that man purse of yours!" Ryan laughed pointing to his fanny pack sitting at his waist.

"Clear out or I'm calling the cops," the man screamed. All of us had heard that before so we turned around and head to our homes.

The next morning I woke up groggier than usual and to my surprise my dad wasn't home. He usually worked night shifts and spent most of his day sleeping on the couch which didn't bother me. As I got dressed I could smell eggs being cooked which meant my mom was home. "Where's Dad?" I asked as I sat down at the kitchen table.

"One of his co-workers had an injury so he got called in for an hour or two until the other man can make it."

Dad was never around for the first part of my life; I actually didn't believe he was my dad when we first met when I was six years old. My mom was the one who always raised me off dad's money, because he was always working in some foreign country.

I shoveled back my breakfast and headed out for another daring day of school. Before I could get out the door my mom yelled, "Jason's picking you up after school. He said he wants to catch up with his little bro."

Jason is my older brother. He's also the only member of the family that understands me, although I never get to see him because he just got out of prison six weeks ago. Why he went I do not know; he wouldn't tell me. All I cared about is I finally get to see him.

The rest of school was slow; I couldn't help but count the hours until I would get to see Jason again.

The final buzzer came and I ran to my locker to grab my skate and Jason was sitting there, arms crossed, leaning against my locker, texting on his old flip phone.

"Jeez, I thought you would've grown up at least a bit by now?" he questioned while he lifted his head from his phone.

"Get off my case. You're the one that's been locked up for six years," I snapped back as I dropped my bag to the floor from my shoulders and gave him a hug.

I grabbed my skate and threw my bag in my locker and walked with my brother to the school doors.

"How's life?" my brother asked.

"How do you think?" I muttered as I shrugged my shoulder. He looked different; it made me wonder what prison does to people. He went in a scrawny kid who liked to wear baggy clothing and skateboard, and now he looked like a gym jockey wearing a skin tight white t-shirt. "Well, let's bring back the old times and I'll film you flipping that thing," my brother said as he made a gesture to my skateboard which was tucked in my arm.

That was probably my favorite childhood memory: my brother filming me skateboarding.

As we walked to the parking lot he reached in his pockets and pulled out a pair of keys and a white car in front of us opened its locks. It was the same car we use to ride in, a 1996 white Honda Civic.

I threw my skate in the over sized trunk and we headed to the old spot we used to skate down the block.

After a short drive that seemed like forever we set up camp at a rail that was beside the entrance to an underground parking lot and I started to skate it with Jason filming my every move. It felt good to have him filming again. He always found the perfect angle.

Hours went by and it was starting to get dark. The last trick I attempted on the rail was a 360 hard flip tail side which is possibly one of the hardest tricks you can do.

Before I hit the rail my board caught on my foot and I fell face first into the pavement. "Ha-ha, that's the best one you've pulled so far!" Jason laughed.

I pulled myself of the ground and Jason was laughing while offering a hand to help me up.

"We should pack up before its get dark out," my brother suggested.

"Yeah, just let me check out that footage."

We sat on the step that I was skating on, he pressed replay on his video camera, and we started to watch the footage.

"Right, before I forget, come with me." My brother was trying to convince me to go to the car with him when I just wanted to watch the film. After arguing, I got off the step and followed him to his car. When we arrived to the empty parking lot he popped his trunk and reached all the way to the back and pulled out a brand new skateboard with a bow on it.

"So now you decide to skateboard with me?" I chuckled.

My brother paused and gave me a puzzled look and then held the skateboard in front of me.

"Happy birthday, little bro." I had been so excited to see my brother I forgot it was my birthday. I took the skate and gave him a brotherly hug.

"So, how about we finish that footage?" he said.

As we were on our way back to the step, an African-American wearing all black walked up to my brother.

"Jason, remember what happened last time you were on my street?" The man said concealing his face except for a nasty scar running down the right side of his lip and a greasy, black beard.

"We don't want trouble he was just film-." Before I could finish he interrupted.

"Filming huh? Hand over the camera J." My brother didn't look frightened.

"And if I don't what are you going to do about it?" My brother snapped back while holding the camera tighter.

The man reached behind his back and pulled something out, but I couldn't make out what it was until he pointed it to my brother. It was a pistol. At this point I was praying it wasn't real. "Ha-ha you're going to shoot me? Is that how you deal with your problems?" Jason laughed.

The man gave Jason a stern look while jamming the gun into his ribs.

"Just give him the camera and let's get the hell out of here," I tried suggesting. Instead of listening to me he grabbed the gun in the man's hand and moved it to his forehead.

"You must have a death wish." The man stuttered while clenching his teeth.

"I'd rather die than cower to you." Jason stated. And before I could react, BANG!

Everything slowed down and I saw my brother fall to the ground in a puddle of his own blood.

"JASON!"

I fell to my knees beside my brother's body and started to cry. The man was already gone and I could hear sirens in the distance.

When the paramedics got there I couldn't move, I was too stunned. It was my birthday and I had just watched my brother get shot in the head.

They took me to the hospital and I sat in the waiting room for hours staring at the white walls with a singular sink in the corner. Finally my mom showed up.

"Honey, I'm so sorry." She said. I couldn't speak, so instead I just hugged her and we both started to cry.

When I got home I washed the blood off the skateboard my brother had given me and hung it up on the wall beside a picture of me and Jason from when I was young. I still couldn't believe he was gone.

The next day I grabbed my skate and headed to school. When I got there I was welcomed by my group of friends who each had a stunned look on his face.

"Johnny, I'm…." Ryan paused.

"Sorry? Being sorry doesn't bring back my brother." I shrugged my shoulder and walked past the group towards my locker.

"Johnny! Hold up!" I snapped my head around and Mikey was running towards me.

"I know it's a bad time for you, but there's a skate competition in Vancouver in a week or two and the group thought it'd be sick if you tagged along." He handed me a flyer and it read "Street skaters aware, the biggest comp is coming back to the big V! Featuring last year's champion Donny Virgo!"

I couldn't believe my eyes. The man that was portrayed as last year's champion was the same man that had shot my brother the previous night. I could see the scar running down his lip and the same musty beard that looked like it was never shaved. I could feel my eyes tearing in anger.

"Johnny, you good?" Mikey asked.

"Do I look good?" I snapped back.

Mikey's face lit up red, without saying a word he walked away.

The only thing that was on my mind was a shot of redemption. Before I let Mikey out of sight I ran after him,

"Yo, Mikey, I'm in!" Mikey turned around and gave me a puzzled look.

"You sure man? You don't have to."

But the thing was, I wanted to.

"When do we leave?" I asked in a stern voice.

He didn't answer, he just looked down at his shoes.

"Is something up?" I questioned again.

"Look at the bottom," he said without looking up. It read:

"Contest takes place June, 29th.."

My jaw dropped to the floor, that would've been Jason's birthday. Now I knew I definitely had to go, for Jason.

Before I could reply to Mikey my phone started to ring. I pulled it out of my pocket and answered it with a common "Hello."

There was no answer.

"Weird," I said as I pressed the hang up button, Mikey was giving me another one of his puzzled looks.

"Telemarketer," I informed him.

He shook his head and walked away. I was ready to call it a day, I went to my locker grabbed my skate and made my way to the parking lot.

When I got their friends were skating on the curb.

"Johnny, check out my front tail!" My friend Ryan popped onto the curb and slid his tail across the whole thing.

I hopped on my skateboard and headed towards the group. My first instinct was to hit the curb.

I hit a simple board slide with a kick flip out.

"J, that was sleazy!" Mikey exclaimed.

All I had my mind set on was doing the laser flip tail slide my brother was filming before he died.

I went back to the start and attempted the trick again. Tthis time when I spun the board my tail slammed into the curb. I flew forward without my board and smashed into the pavement.

"Damn that was close! What trick was that?" Ryan yelled.

"The trick I was telling you about. It's the last trick I tried before my brother died."

Ryan gave me sympathetic look and put his hand on my shoulder,

"I'm really sorry, man." I could feel my eyes starting to tear and instead of letting them show, I popped my skate into my hands and started to head home.

The street I ride on is always slow. You'll be lucky if you see anyone walking or driving there, but that was fine with me. The quiet gave me time to clear my head and that's what I really needed.

I still couldn't believe Jason was gone, and to add to it, the man who killed him was the champion of the comp in Vancouver.

But that didn't bother me, the thing that bothered me is I was never going to see Jason again, and the competition is only in a few weeks and I don't feel ready.

And I don't know how good this guy who shot Jason even is. He had to be good if he won the competition last year.

And then I thought about it. The man that killed my brother is the champion of a local skate competition. That's how I would avenge my brother. Instead of relying on violence, I was going to take his title. It wouldn't be easy though, but if I can land my 360 hard flip tail slide, that title would be mine.

So with no hesitation I pulled out my phone and dialed Ryan's number.

"Yo, J what's good?" He answered.

"Yo I need you to drive me to Vancouver. Could you do that?" There was a brief silence and then he said as long as I pay for gas everything's all good, but I had no money.

After Ryan hung up I dialed Rob's number, but when he answered he seemed mad.

"What's up man you sound mad. Everything good?" I asked.

"Yeah, me and my dad just got into a fight, but it's all good. What do you need? Let me guess you called to ask for a ride?" I don't know how, but he guessed it on the dot.

"You need a board too, don't you?" He added.

"Only if you're offering," I replied.

Again there was a brief silence and then he said, "Hey man, you know I got you covered. I'll talk to you later."

I slid my phone back into my pocket and picked up speed, but something caught my attention. A little kid was being held up by an older kid. I immediately thought this could be a way to vent my stress

"Give me your money you little puke!" The older kid snapped.

This kid was wearing a light blue t shirt with white jeans and was roughly the same size as me, which made me wonder why he was picking on a little kid.

Something told me to keep rolling by, but I couldn't be a bystander. Besides, that could've been me when I was young, so I made my way to the scene.

When I got there the kids didn't even notice me.

"If he's the little puke in this situation, then we must be living in an alternate universe," I muttered.

The older kid turned his head and glared at me. He looked confused, but still didn't let go of the kid.

"Drop the kid or else I drop you," I stated.

The bully let go of the kid and started to laugh.

"You think this is funny?" I snapped.

The smile on his face instantly turned into a frown. "You want to get hit, punk?" The kid asked.

"Funny, I was about to ask you the same question."

And that's when his arm started to move swiftly towards my face. I've been in a lot of fights and Jason taught me a few things, so before he could connect I grabbed his elbow and threw my fist.

It hit with a smack against his cheek and some blood flew from his mouth. I threw a strong uppercut and it caught the kid right on the chin causing him to stumble against the brick wall. Before he could retaliate I grabbed his shirt and hoisted him off the ground against the wall.

"How much money did he take?" I asked the little boy while glancing at him.

"None, because you showed up."

Through the boys tears I could see a smile unfolding. I looked back at the older kid, who had blood pouring out his mouth onto my clothes,

"What pocket is your money in?" I asked the bully.

No answer. I looked to his jean pockets and I saw a green paper sticking out. As I went to reach for his pockets, he grabbed my wrist.

I threw one last slug and it knocked him unconscious, causing him to fall to the concrete.

I reached into his pocket and pulled out two twenty dollar bills.

I pocketed one and gave the other one to the little boy.

"Go home before his friends show up to bully you some more," I suggested.

The little boy folded the twenty into his pocket, hugged me, ran away, and disappeared behind the corner.

I looked at the now conscious kid lying on the ground. I pinned my knees to his arm and wound up for a swing, but right before I connected my phone started to ring causing me to pause.

It was the same number from in the school that never answered.

"Hello," I answered.

"I wouldn't do that if I were you." A familiar, creepy voice stated.

"Who is this?" I asked frantically while getting of the boy.

"Johnny, do you think hitting that kid would make your dead brother Jason proud?"

I wanted to reply but I couldn't, instead I dropped the phone and started to cry. I grabbed the phone of the ground and spoke. "Who are you?"

I heard the sound of a telephone hanging up. I grabbed my skateboard and continued to my house.

When I walked through the door of my apartment my mom's jaw dropped.

"Honey, what happened?! Are you okay?" She panicked while grabbing my shirt to get a closer look at the blood.

"There was a disagreement," I said while shrugging my mom's hand off.

"Honey, you can't do this! You don't want to end up like your brother."

I glanced my head down to my shirt which was covered in blood, and before she could say something else I interrupted, "Why'd he get locked up? And don't bother trying to lie to me like you have my whole life."

My mom began to cry which didn't bother me. In my mind she deserved it, but there was still something about the guy who shot my brother, how did he know him from before? The words: "Jason, remember what happened last time you were on my street?" pulsed through my head. Why was that man calling me and how did he know who Jason was?

"He was framed after one of his friends was shot. You don't remember?" My mom stuttered.

And it all came back to me. My brother was taking me home when the cops pulled him over and found a gun that he claimed wasn't his, but it all made sense now. And Donny's title was mine.

The next morning I woke up to it raining outside. I grabbed my phone of the dresser and dialed Rob's number. When he answered he seemed like he was tired. "You better wake up because we're heading to the big V today." I taunted

"Yeah man I'll be at your house in like an hour to pick you up, is that cool?"

"Perfect." I responded.

The day was finally here. I looked at the picture of me and Jason hanging up on my wall and almost started to cry. I looked at the board he had given me which was hanging crooked on my wall and glanced at my current one that was thrashed from all the skating it's been through. Without a second guess I grabbed my new skateboard and waited for Rob.

When Rob arrived I was waiting on the sidewalk practicing my kick flips.

"Jump in!" Rob said with a grin.

I grabbed my skateboard and jumped in the back of his white mini van.

Veronica:

Wild Groves is an incomplete 12,000 word mystery thriller novella. Wild Groves is the definition of a quiet, safe boring town; that is, until Laura's friend is murdered shocking everyone. Laura must do anything to find out who the killer, even if the killer turns out to be more psychotic than she expects. This crime thriller is set in a town where nothing bad ever happens, but even the safest towns have secrets...

Wild Groves

The merry jingle of the bell above the small door shook ever so slightly as Laura Denvers entered the tiny isolated bakery, escaping the early morning rush of workers bustling outside.

The sweet smells of fresh homemade pastries instantly wafted up her nose as she shook off the light snow that began to coat her midnight blue cashmere sweater. She silently cursed herself for not bringing a jacket instead. The coldness from outside began to melt away like a Hershey kiss left out in the sun.

Laura decided on a small table at the front, so she could be closer to her good friend Ginny, who ran the bakery with her family.

The nearing 8:00 a.m. hour brought only a few regular customers for their early morning breakfast fix, so Laura pretty much had the whole bakery to herself.

Wondering if Ginny was working, Laura abandoned her black purse and red winter hat at the table and made her way to the front counter which was decorated in various Christmas decorations since Christmas was next week. Oh how Wild Grove loved their Christmas thought Laura, a smile creeping up her lips.

Laura also had noticed a new hand drawn sign that read 'check out our latest Christmas menu' which was displayed at the back wall behind the counter.

Mmmm. Laura could feel her mouth start to salivate as she read the various Christmas specials like 'Santa's caramel surprise' or Rudolph's velvet cake'. Her eyes also scanned the winter specials which were right beside the Christmas specials. Her eyes landed on Caramel spiced lattes and apple cinnamon crumble cakes which were some of her favorites.

Laura could feel her stomach growling like an African lion, a reminder that she hadn't eaten breakfast that morning.

Upon her arrival to the counter, she expected at least Ginny's parents, Mrs. and Mr. Turnvil to greet her, as they usually catered to the early customers. But there was no sign of Ginny, her aunts, cousins or her parents anywhere. This was odd.

Just as if her thoughts had been answered, Ginny walked through the double doors from the back, carrying a bowl of something secretive and wearing the usual Wild Grove bakery attire, which consisted of a white apron that read 'Wild Grove bakery is the best' and a chef hat with a tree drawn on it.

"Hey Laura, long time no see! How are you doing?" Ginny called happily.

"Oh I'm okay, just been really busy with work at the office and you know the usual." Which meant working at the popular newspaper office downtown, going home to her family, and catering to her three dogs.

"Wow, you have been quite the busy bee," Ginny said setting down the bowl which smelled like something fruity.

"Yea, how about yourself?"

"Oh I've been good. With the bakery and you know the family it's been pretty hectic, especially with the holidays coming around."

"Tell me about it," Laura said chuckling softly; her grandparents were coming up from New York tomorrow and her sister and brother were flying down as well. And the house was still a mess.

"So anyways, would you mind coming out back and helping me sort this recipe before, you know, my mom comes, and starts yelling at me." Ginny hoisted the bowl, leaving brown batter all over the counter.

"Sure, no problem!" Laura said following Ginny into the back.

An aroma of sweet cookies and pastries was in the air as they stepped through the wide double doors. The blanket feel of the warmth was bliss.

Laura loved the eighteenth century feel to the building. It was historical and all the secrets that this building must have and imagining all the people that must have gone through those double doors was magical. She thought about this every time she set foot in the bakery, especially now seeing the old stove oven and high ceiling where the Turnvils worked.

"Smells nice," Laura said, reaching for an apron from the many hooks dangling on the walls.

"You say that every time," Ginny laughed while teasingly rolling her eyes.

"Well, try living in my house, it constantly smells like wet dog."

"Only if you try living with my annoying cousins"

"Okay fine, deal."

"Wait. What's a deal?" Benny, Ginny's oldest cousin, said walking in.

"Uhhh nothing," Laura said quickly, blushing since she had a thing for Benny.

"Ya, we…um…were just talking about how much we like love winter and all…" Ginny stuttered.

"Oh spare me, Ginny. You've hated winter for as long as I can remember. And you too Laura"

At the mention of her name, Laura blushed even brighter, if that was possible. Benny was twenty-six and four years older than she and Ginny. She had first met him six years ago when he had moved up from Turkey with Ginny and his family.

"No, I've never said that I've hated winter. I just don't like the cold and the slush on the streets."

"Sure okay, even though I remember specifically you telling me you really hated winter"

"No, I haven't! Okay when then? Huh?"

Ginny continued to argue with Benny. They acted like brother and sister, having grown up with each other and all. Ginny had always wondered why Laura even had a crush on Benny since he was annoying and in her words 'immature,' but Laura couldn't help it, one look in to those green honey eyes and she was a goner.

"Okay how about last week at Nana's? Does that ring any bells"

"No and you ver-"

"Guys be quiet. I can hear you from all the way back here," Benny's mom, Patricia said, walking in.

"Sorry, Mama," Benny said quickly and Laura found herself liking him even more.

"Benny dear, go out back and help unload the dishware and you two stop playing around and get back to sorting that batter before I tell your mother, Ginny." She looked at Ginny from underneath her glasses.

"Yes, Patricia," Ginny said. If there was one person who she was afraid of, it was Patricia. She looked like an innocent woman from the outside, but on the inside she was fierce and wasn't afraid of showing it.

After Benny had walked away Patricia turned to Laura and smiled warmly.

"Oh my dear, sorry. Didn't mean to shout at ya. What are you even doing helping Ginny? She is very well capable herself, aren't you?" Patricia said turning to Ginny sternly.

"Yes, Patricia." Ginny said continuing to separate the dough into even balls on the tinfoil.

"How are you? I miss seeing you around here and how about your mom?"

"Oh she's good and I'm good thanks, how about yourself?"

Laura began to blush that the attention had turned to her again, especially since it was Benny's mom.

"Oh, I'm good dear. Tell your mom I say hi, I have to go and see if Benny isn't breaking anything," she chuckled, and with that she was off.

"Ughhh I really dislike her, you know." Ginny said, after she was out of earshot.

"Come on, you don't really mean that right? Even though she is really strict with you... but you know she only means well since she loves you very much."

"Oh stop it; you're starting to sound like my mother."

"I'm just trying to help, Ginns"

"Ya well you can find a different way to help, like maybe going to the store and getting me a bigger tip to decorate these cookies"

"Okay if that helps, but you know your aunt does love you."

"Get going before I throw up. I hate gushy stuff" Ginny replied laughing

"Okay okay, I'm going."

"Better hurry up before Benny leaves," Ginny said making kissing sounds like a person younger than twenty two.

"Shut up." Laura said blushing like a tomato; yet again.

"You know I'm right, hunny" Ginny said continuing to laugh and separate batter.

"I'm leaving now. I'll see you in a bit."

And with that Laura turned on her heels and was out the door before Ginny could tease her even more.

As soon as Laura stepped into the cold wintery air, she could feel the coldness melting away any warmth that she had from the warm bakery. Still cursing herself for not bringing a coat, she began her short descent to the dollar store that was only a couple stores down.

Wild Grove was bustling with life, like usual at such an early hour. There were people swarming all about, probably for the Christmas parade that was rolling in next week. Wild Grove was a nice quaint old town of about ten thousand people. It wasn't extremely huge, but not too small either. That's why Laura also liked Wild Grove.

She had grown up in a town far away called Glassendale. She had truly loved Glassendale, but wanted to move out and spread her wings like some people would say and go to Wild Grove College. This worked out, since her aunt lived in Wild Grove, but five years ago tragic struck and her dad sold their house and moved in with Ginny in the wake of her mother's death , there wasn't a day that went by that Laura didn't think of her mom.

Laura was frustrated about moving but in the end it all worked out because she liked having her dad live with her and she enjoyed Wild Grove; it was a safe nice town. Nothing ever happened in Wild Grove, and Laura liked it that way.

Daisy's Dollar store was an old building just like the rest, at the end of the street and followed by a huge field behind and on one side of it. Nobody ventured this far off in town and some said that Daisy's Dollar store was haunted. Normally Laura didn't believe in such superstitions and myths, but today she had an odd feeling of being watched.

Daisy's Dollar Store had seen better days. Now it donned brown peeling paint at the front and a poorly painted sign that had the words fading. Nobody was outside milling about and the wind seemed to howl like a ghost. Laura stepped up on the porch frightened by the squeaking of the wood which made her feel foolish. *It's just a porch and there are no such things as ghosts!* she thought to herself.

Hurriedly Laura bounded inside, to find the place completely empty... That was odd. The owner Shelly wouldn't just leave the door unlocked if the store wasn't open! And the store was usually opened on Monday mornings. This was odd.

Laura reached for the light switch beside the door and was instantly blinded for a couple of seconds by the sheer brightness. Once she composed herself she called out to the owner,

No reply, not even a sound..

Okay this is was definitely weird. Just as Laura was about to step out and rid herself of the spookiness that lay about she heard a sound.

It sounded like a hammer on a nail, and it was coming from the back of the room. Laura debated whether she should follow it or seriously just go back and tell Ginny and Benny about it. Benny, she thought as her heart beat quickened. Such a stupid time to be thinking of a boy she thought angrily. Before she could even react she heard a man's voice call out, "Who's there?"

Laura responded trying to sound brave and firm. It didn't really work out, as her voice squeaked at the end. "I'm looking for Shelly. What are you doing here?'

The man responded after a couple of moments, probably debating what to say. Laura could feel her palms start to sweat and wondered if the man was still even there. But surely the man spoke, in a deep gruff voice.

"I'm the construction worker Shelly hired and I don't know where she is."

"How can I be sure that what you're saying is true, Shelly wouldn't just leave her shop unattended" Laura found herself saying without even thinking.

The man laughed, a horrible wheezing sound and Laura found herself cringing. He finally stopped and said, "What are you, a detective? She's at home and she told me to do construction so she can open up soon."

"Then why is the door unlocked? And why aren't there more workers?" Laura replied, gaining confidence as she spoke.

"Boy, you sure ask a lot of questions. I accidently forgot to lock the door, and I'm the only maintenance guy she could find at this time of year. You know, since it's close to the holidays..."

Laura thought hard about what she should say next. She couldn't tell if he was lying or not. She would have to see him first. "Why don't you show yourself?"

There was a scuttling noise as if the man was rearranging something. Laura grabbed the nearest object she could find, which was a mug that could double as a weapon if needed. The only other time that she had felt in grave danger was when she went camping with her two best friends to Lake Wickinowa four years ago. They had been seriously contemplating if the whole place was just haunted because of a series of mishaps. But in fact it just turned out to be some of the neighboring campers who liked to play jokes.

But this was real and Laura hoped to god that the man was not an axe murderer. The scuttling noise had stopped and the loud noise of silence gave her an eerie feeling.

"Hello, are you still there?" Laura called out, her heart thumping violently in her chest.

"Sorry to scare ya, I had to quickly apply the shiner for the wallpaper."

The man spoke again with a gruff voice, stepping into the light.

The man was surprisingly tall and looked to be in his early fifties; his brown graying hair was greasy looking and combed back like he had used some sort of styling product. He wore a long sleeve shirt that was so dirty you couldn't even tell what color it had been once. His pants were long and grazed the bottom of his dirty black boots. His looks weren't startling but his blue intense eyes stole the show. They were hard and Laura found it difficult to maintain eye contact with the man. Laura remembered something she had heard somewhere, that eyes are the windows to the soul. In this case she wondered what the old man had seen. Laura's eyes traveled down to his hands where he held a hammer.

Laura gripped her mug hard in case she needed to use it, but what was a mug to a hammer? As if the man read her mind he set down the hammer on the nearest table and spoke. "No need to be scared Miss; I'm just a regular maintenance man." As he spoke his eyes never once left Laura's face.

"Who said I'm scared?" Laura said calmly setting the mug down.

The man didn't speak, but instead walked closer, until he was a couple feet away and then surprisingly smiled, an evil smile that looked like it had been carved in with a knife.

Although before the man could speak his phone rang, "Hold on I have to take this" he said answering and then turned around and walked back to the back of the room.

In a split second, Laura decided to walk back to the bakery. She grabbed the nearest bag of cupcake decorating tips and speed walked outside, hoping the man wouldn't notice. S he decided that she would pay Shelly back later for her unplanned thievery.

A couple of minutes later she found herself back at the bakery, rushing inside almost knocking into a couple of customers at the entrance. "Sorry," she said as they eyed her angrily. She then spotted Ginny at the front counter catering to customers; which was strange, as usually Benny's mom catered to them.

"Hey psst Ginny, I need to talk to you!" Laura said side stepping customers at the front counter.

"Oh thank god Laura, I do too! "

"Wait, you do?"

"Yes but I'll explain as soon as I get Benny to cater the front, hold on I'll be back," she said both to Laura and the customers; as she hurried to the back and went through the double doors.

It felt forever until Ginny returned but it was probably only a couple seconds. When she stepped through with Benny, Laura's heart skipped a beat and she found herself smiling at him, which for some reason he didn't return.

"Okay, Laura, I need you to listen to me, what did you see at Shelly's store?"

Laura was taken aback as she eyed Ginny with wide eyes.

"Um that's what I was just going to tell you! There was a strange man in there and…" but before she could finish Ginny covered her mouth in horror.

"What, what's wrong?! Ginny... Please tell me!" Laura found herself saying as she grabbed Ginny by the shoulders.

Ginny grabbed hold of Laura's arm and pulled her further to the back of the room, ignoring the people's stares as they went by. When they found a secluded corner at the back of the room she finally spoke.

"Okay listen to me, even if you want to ask a question, don't interrupt, okay?" Ginny said her eyes growing wide.

"Okay, okay I won't," Laura said, finding everything very strange.

"Okay good, well yesterday," Ginny paused to look around and then continued, "Yesterday the police said that Shelly was murdered and they suspect the man or actually they suspect that it's two men and- Laura forgot her promise to not interrupt and spoke.

"What, Shelly was murdered!?"Laura said her eyes wide, "but but..."

Laura had been close to death before, for years she tried to deny the death of her mother and the only people she had turned to had been Ginny and Shelly. Shelly was the kindest soul on the planet that wouldn't even harm a fly, and was like a second mother to Laura, having met her when she moved to Wild Grove from Glassendale a couple years ago.

"Yes. I wouldn't lie about this..." Ginny said as Laura's eyes widened even more if that was possible. Then Ginny began to twirl her hair which was a habit of hers when she was thinking.

"Like I said, when I was at Shelly's just now, well I saw a man and…"

"But the police said they were just there and…"

"I did hear him hammering something out back so maybe he could have been hiding from them?"

"Hmm. That could be a possibility," Ginny said looking around again, as if the very killers were around.

"They recovered Shelly's body by the river by two pines this morning," Ginny said looking down sadly.

"But didn't they track any foot prints in the snow or something?" Laura said thinking aloud.

"Now that you mention that... no which is the strangest thing..."

Just then Laura's eyes widened, matching Ginny's.

"Maybe they took the old pipes that run underneath Shelly's shop?"

Ginny began to twirl her hair harder as she spoke

"You're absolutely right! But wait, aren't they blocked off?"

"Yes, but you can always use a crowbar. They are usually shielded away and only a local would know where to look... So it could be possible that the police couldn't see it."

"Couldn't see what?" a man's voice boomed from behind, both Ginny and Laura jumped as they whipped around to see who had spoken.

Standing there was a police officer wearing a serious expression.

"Oh, hey officer." Ginny spoke first. "Um...we were just talking about what had happened to Shelly."

"Wouldn't surprise me, I suspect Wild Grove hasn't had a crime this big in a long time."

"Yes sir. The last one was when my grandmother was just a little girl," Laura said, looking away from the police officer's intense stare.

"Now, I heard you saying something about some old pipes. I'm not from around here. Where did you say they connect from?"

Both Laura and Ginny looked at each other.

The police officer looked odd, his clothes were ruffled and she was sure that his badge didn't resemble anything close to the logo of the police men around Wild Grove. His clothes were covered in rusted spots that she hoped wasn't blood. Laura didn't know if they should trust him and say anything. But before she could do anything Ginny spoke.

"They connect to Shelly's place sir."

"Oh, I see" the police officer said putting a hand to his chin to think.

"Will you ladies excuse me? I just have to go out front to tell the other officers."

"Ya sure," Ginny said as the man began to walk back out the entrance door.

As soon as he had disappeared. Laura turned to Ginny, "Maybe we shouldn't have told him anything?"

"Why not? He was a police officer."

"Because, come on, didn't he look sort of…? I don't know weird? Like he didn't know what he was doing? Come on, Ginny he didn't even have a walkie talkie… I mean, don't most police officers carry one? And did you see his badg-"

"Oh Laura, you worry way too much." Ginny interrupted simply looking at her cracked nail polish.

"Ugh I should really get a manicure."

"A manicure?! Gin stay on topic here… And we don't even know if they're police officers from around here working on this case. They tend to stick to the smaller crimes."

"Fine, but first let's eat, because I'm starving" Ginny patted her stomach and then glanced at the cupcake decorating tips that Laura held in her hand.

"Wow, you actually got the tips? But how-"

"When I ran away I just took the bag, because I knew how much you need them and I can always pay..." Laura looked down and began to cry,

"You were going to say Shelly right?" Ginny spoke for her.

"Yeah, I just can't believe that she's actually gone. I had just seen her about three days ago... all full of life and then one day she's just not..." Laura sat down and began to wipe her face.

She couldn't understand why the most beautiful souls died.. She knew people sometimes said that things happen for a reason, but why her mom who was still so young and why Shelly? Why all the other beautiful people that had died? One time four years ago, a couple days after her mother's death, she remembered vividly like it had just been yesterday, that she had stood crying with Shelly and she remembered asking her why god had taken her mother from her and why did the most pretty goodhearted people die? That's when Shelly had taken her hands in hers and as an example used a garden and asked her if she were to walk into a breathtaking garden bursting with flowers, which flowers would she pick? The pretty ones? Or the ones that were dying and shriveled up? Laura remembered saying that she would pick the beautiful ones, and that's when Shelly had said "Exactly." Those words had stuck with

Laura throughout the years and she often found herself repeating the words in her head.

"Well she's in a better place now and I know that's what everybody says, but it's the truth... and you know how much she would talk about one day being with god upstairs," Ginny said making Laura snap out of her thoughts.

Ginny took a seat beside Laura and Laura could smell her rose perfume that was a comforting scent.

"Yeah, but it's not fair she...."

"Laura, sometimes life isn't fair and that's just the way it goes, like it or not."

"Wow, you sound like Benny's mom," Laura said laughing while wiping her stuffy nose, and then more tears began to fall like a waterfall, As the thoughts and memories of Shelly and her mother flooded through her thoughts. Although she had never gotten that expression, because if your tears fell like a waterfall... well then they would be covered with water right now and even though it was just a figure of speaking, Laura had always found it weird.

"Oh god, I do sound like her." Ginny said laughing along while standing up.

"I know a way to help you feel better!"

"Okay what is it?" Laura said smiling up at Ginny and finally realizing how empty the place had become... I guess word had spread quite fast, Laura thought to herself.

Garrett:

The Depths is an incomplete 110,000 word adventure novel. Xandria's psychotic mental health complications throw her over the edge, sending her into a dimension between two existences where everything is surreal and no one is normal. The new world seems like an enjoyable place, but strange recurring events beginning to take place alter that vision as she travels endless frightening caverns and eventually reunites with a fallen best friend.

The Depths

Psychosis

The ultimate destination lay ahead, where every positive memory had been enslaved and cast into the wilting remains of a two-hundred-foot silo. She longed to reach its highest balcony, sprinting through the derelict golden field creeping up to its base. Sixteen interconnected cylinders were all that stood between herself and eternal reprieve.

"You won't be any more after this," she huffed, referring to the voice inside: Charlie, as she had named him. His words paved every moment endured throughout her life: the multiple personas and pitches, desires and commands. Without them, she would exist without feelings, emotions, or most of all the desire to end everything: the same desire enforced by the disappearance of her best friend Emily just two years prior.

Despite the things people would say, the one who knew her most meant everything. They would say that he was merely a product of her imagination, and those unable to comprehend his presence would consider him as an 'imaginary friend', disconcerting her with the fact that his words catalyzed the little that she was capable of feeling.

You had to come here because everyone hates us. We cannot escape them.

Her muscles tore with terminal motivation: she arrived at the base, pinning herself against the concrete with an endless stream of desperate gasps and solemn tears scraping her face. Emily and herself had built an opening together, and it was hidden nearby beneath the shadow of four separate containers.

Remember how you two angels trespassed, just so you could be here? It's so you could find a way inside because that's how much anyone cared about you.

She grabbed the veil of black hugging both sides of her face, collapsing into dry mud and wailing. "It's the only enjoyable place we had!"

You're just brutally unloved! Left to fester all because of what they called an accident!

The local headline from that day flashed across her mind: Two Vehicle Collision: Parents and Daughter Deceased. "They killed her!" She thrust her face into the dirt, dousing the voice momentarily. Picking herself back up: she grabbed her face, glancing around through her fingers while struggling to regain balance. A differentiated pair of red and white orbs filled in her vision, throwing the surrounding world from its equilibrium. Her back was caught by the concrete wall as an unmerciful shrill rang around her: she forced both eyes shut; *Everyone only cares about killing you and there's only one way to get away!*

The teen dashed through a nearby gap making up the structure. *Go, to the top, quickly!* The once playful voice had become no more, having evolved itself into worsening thoughts and aggravation. Fear for her own sanity powered her obedience as she listened to everything he had to say, along with a persistent screeching coming from the distance. She stumbled into an enclosed junction with their narrow opening crumbled into one convex wall, crashing through it with crunchy footsteps vanishing into the limitless overhead. *It's just up there, so close yet so far – just like every dream or aspiration you've ever had.*

Several whispers encircled her with countless tones: *You're worthless! Useless!*

She reached into her jeans with trembling hands, pulling out the thin smartphone which displayed the same wallpaper that had remained unchanged for two years: Emily and Xandria, holding their heads together with unforgettable grins splashed across both faces.

You two were pathetic together like that.

"The only friend I've ever had!" She screamed, sending the device into the floor and throwing herself with it. Her mouth filled with dust as she began the struggle to locate her phone, having the familiar pair come into focus just out of arms' reach, but with a new cobweb of cracks spread across the display.

I knew that's how you've thought of her all along!

"Shut up!" She demanded, grabbing her head. "Just shut up!"

You very well know that there's only one way to make me shut up, the voice contrived with reassurance in his tone.

Pressing her head together diffused some pressure, but any memory of Emily was nothing to be forgotten. She had shattered what was displaying their final photo from that life changing day, and with it went what used to be their main form of communication. Xandria picked the device back up, dragging the notification tray across roughened glass to illuminate the flashlight.

The hauntingly familiar haven of concrete and dust adorned with ancient steel catwalks loomed above, missing one key sense of security: *That same person you never cared for in the first place.*

She sighed, gazing into the memory of herself alongside Emily, enjoying their company without insight towards what would happen just hours later. One unmistakable smile; the other, extinguished. Those bright eye contrasted her own complexion, along with her dark hair intermingling with Emily's immaculate stretch of blonde. The photo was all that remained after giving her friend the Micro SD card that day, and there was no way to carry on. Drops formed at the bridge of her nose as she pushed up her small body, submitting to an outburst of enclosed tears. The One Within possessed no remorse for her cries: *Just throw yourself down like you did to her. She only cared about you because she was just like you, without friends aside from you!*

"Emily cared about me because we were perfect together!"

No, because the two of you were downright scum! Her mind lowered its tone, continuing to bark away at every remaining fragment of sanity. *You can do this. Now get yourself up, and carry on.*

She obeyed his false calamity, stifling a cough and patting parched dust from her maroon pullover. The phone in hand taunted her with the same image that drove the voice. "I'm doing this for you, Emily," she whispered, thumbing away some powder from the cobweb of cracks. "I'll be with you again."

Yes, you will be ... in her arms again. Just like in that thing you destroyed.

Her otherwise scattered mind remained at mercy of the voice despite recognizing his incessant manipulation. "I will once again be in your arms."

A sudden blast from behind sent her entire body into shivering. Fear for herself and the opportunity to somehow reunite with Emily consumed her, driven by concurrent hisses coming from the same ambience, eventually converting themselves into noise: the roar of an engine woke up in the distance, piling fear deep into her chest. Vehicles seemed to begin whizzing about without particular direction or origin, drowning her with an orchestra of fiery combustion and screeching. Two bright blue headlights cleared the distance, cementing themselves in place yet speeding directly towards her.

A pair of hands grasped her sides, forcing her to remain frozen in the lamps' direct path. She wished to scream, to emphasize her grasp on reality, but there was none: she was being held hostage to her own mind. A tire screaming upon disused tarmac flew by, infusing her entirety with the same fear holding her in place.

It's coming to get you! The One Within shouted. He repeated himself, conjuring a sphere of burning rubber and restless growls around her head, closing in on her small slouched form. An implosion echoed from afar, recovering memories of the life changing night. The piercing noises all around were approaching too quickly, breaking next to her with another blast of shattered glass and twisted steel scattering about without indication of presence.

This is exactly what you did with the only memory you've got left of her!

Shutting both eyes for a moment ceased the action: they fluttered open, blinding her with the same pair of headlamps which had stopped directly ahead.

Sweetheart... Now you get to see what you did to her.

Her heart hammered within her ears: she was greeted with two conglomerations of mangled steel cast at each side. An innocent looking beer bottle taunted her from the dust, leading to several more directing her eyes towards a classic black Jaguar pinned to its side with the sunroof torn through. A young man was trapped inside, directing a pair of dead eyes into her own; "Turn around," he murmured with his head jittering for the last time. "This would have never happened ... if they never touched that beer."

She forced her way through the shock by nodding at him, beginning to turn around before being interrupted.

That's how much anyone cares about you. That guy knows everything you're about to deal with, but he didn't mention it.

"Just don't do anything else," she whimpered. Tears pushed their way through: "Please... I'll do anything for ... for you to just ... just leave."

It's too late now. You came knowing very well what you want. Now look at what he told you to look at.

She sniffled under persuasion from the voice.

Go on. Just on your left. Everything you've ever wished for.

Her eyes darted around, stopping at the old topless Jeep that never failed to entrance her with its vintage charm, resting on the left side and wafting away the yeasty aroma of cheap lager. The vehicle remained vacant until he released a demonic gnarl, casting a red aura inside to reveal a motionless set of three: the disdainful couple of which she despised, strapped in with only their seatbelts. The person sitting behind stole all air from her lungs. "Em!" She cried, inducing life upon the trio: they looked up at her in the same barren manner as the person beforehand, but their faces consisted of nothing more than carelessly embalmed sections of a corpse.

Shattered, destroyed! Look! It's what you did to her!

Xandria forced herself up, but was unable to stay. Her face contorted with the reaction, pushing her mouth open to unleash all the turmoil within: she locked out her senses, tearing apart her throat from inside. The hidden face of her fallen best friend would not disappear from memory, until a gentle hand was brushed down her arm, choking into silence: "You have nothing to worry about anymore," he stated. Both eyes shot open, finding nothing more than the familiar dark calamity illuminated by the phone at her side. She began gasping for air, grasping her confused head without certainty of the location.

It's all inside you, like everyone always says.

Her mind was eased with his reversion to a regular tone, but the change in pitch was unable to reverse the turmoil that he had imposed. Attempting to speak brought nothing; instead, the girl's tremoring hands retrieved the device, peering into the same untouchable smiles as before, though something about them was strange: their mouths seemed to move, calling out to her by flashing into a row of serrated lit up by deep amber hues replacing their eyes. "Useless!" The voice growled in a new hellish tone.

She shuddered backwards, flinging the phone away. "Leave me alone!"

I'm not going to leave you alone until you're done for!

The alteration was nothing more than another mind trick: she retrieved the phone right away, using her other hand to push away some tear soaked dust encrusted upon her face. The precious photo cast security from its backlight, causing her to grasp the phone with everything while continuing along her final motive. Ambient light cast through from outside brightened a steel stairwell next to the hole that they had broken, having remained untouched over the years. The ascent appeared rickety and dangerous but there was no concern. Her only aspiration laid within the blackness above.

"Now move yourself!" The persistent voice commanded from all around, fueling the raging torment within. She ran up and tripped into the first set of handrails, rattling the world around and coughing up the impact. Her balance diminished once again, flipping her stomach. She held the phone against her chest, holding the rough railing with everything she had. Several deep breaths stabilized her queasy innards, cooling off her heated body before turning around along the same path as before.

She began dashing up endless flights of treacherous stairs. The entire passage was indifferent the entire way up with nothing averting her from the inevitable. She eventually crossed paths with a cracked door, stopping herself by slamming into the opposing wall. She stumbled, overtaken by the desperation for any distraction. As she forced herself around and through the door, its ancient hinges creaked open, leading to the grimy remains of a small lavatory which had not been used for many years.

Her attention was caught by a white point reflecting from the wall: she directed her phone into it, meeting with a dust coated mirror hung above a sink filled with forgotten building hardware. The girl groaned, pushing herself towards the basin and using her wrist to wipe away some old dirt. A pristine glass pane hid beneath, casting the reflection of a small pathetic face that seemed to glare back at herself. Raising the flashlight, her pair of sunken eyes lit up, shadowed by thick black hair. They seemed to be despising their coexistence, the reflected form against the physical one.

"So this is what you've become," she commented, brushing aside a dense cluster of strands. "Allowing yourself to be controlled by that thing in your head."

You're talking to me while talking to yourself, he sneered.

"No, I'm not talking to you," she responded, leaning into the glass while wiping away some fresh tears. "I'm talking to you, Xandria."

She spent some time with herself, staring at the reflection, unable to lift the small frown consisting of her lips. Another tear fell, staining her eye with unmitigated remorse. Lowering the phone: "If only I was like everyone else."

But you're not like those people, you're really not.

Charlie was attempting to console her, but the previous assault was too much: submitting to his motivation was only possible through forced misery. "If only you could get outside of me somehow," she sighed.

He slowed his voice. *You want to see me ... outside ...?*

She yelped with indication of what was coming. Her own face pulled in all attention: she stepped back, finding something tickling its way up the back of her head. "Please ... don't do it..."

Liquid heat began oozing out the top of her head. A pair of curled charcoal points began pushing their way through, encapsulating her burning face within an orb of red. The radiant horns pressed forward, setting on their dreadful journey towards her pupils. They continued as a lanky black pair of hands slithered by from behind, wrapping themselves around her chest. Their fingertips pressed themselves inside, pulling away from one another while her vision was displaced by the horns. The undetectable tar from her head oozed down, adhering her shoes to the floor.

This is exactly what you've wanted this entire time! He shrilled, entrapping her head within a circle of warped laughter.

Her body crumbled into the dusty floor with her screams being drowned out by the melody of distasteful cackles. Pulling both hands to her face: she continued wailing through suffocation, sealing her eyes against the presence of Charlie who had frozen time. Her chest imploded by the heat of surrounding flames, forcing both eyes open to meet a furious crimson black inferno which was consuming the room.

Her throat ruptured again as she cancelled out the surroundings approaching her body. Smoke stung her nostrils, and she began burning alive; it's all done for, but it's what you wanted, he whispered, immediately extinguishing his attack. *Open your eyes now. Nothing happened.*

Under the Inner One's mercy: the girl widened both eyes, coming to the same photo resting in her hand with the same taunting web of glass separating it from the outside world. She found herself slouched against concrete, sitting across from the sink and mirror. Several tears fell down, rushing to her lips before being wiped away.

Did you forget about why you came here?

Her desire of showing no mercy had been consumed by terrorizing fear. She trembled upwards, holding the phone against her heart and starting towards the oxidized door.

Do I have to remind you again, about what your purpose is?

Her chest began hammering against the picture. "You won't do that to me again!" She commanded. "I'm the one in control now!"

Then prove it to me! Prove to me that you don't need me anymore!

She had lost everything: her best friend, along with the motivation to endure the surprises that another day would bring. Her family meant nothing, and society consisted of nothing more than pawns being ruled by the same world that denied her the right to fit in. She forced herself out of the forgotten room, continuing the furious clamoring of footsteps along neglected steel, though not for much longer as the exit drew near. Just a handful of steps remained: the memory in her hand pushed her along. *I'm doing this for you,* the teen thought, immersing herself with the phone upon reaching a jarred door concluding her ascent. "You were all the good that this planet had to offer."

She pushed the metal door aside, presenting her entire life ahead: Sebring, the place she grew up, and where was tossed around like an unwanted gift with each passing day. An intricate labyrinth of lamps and buildings dawned upon her as she walked to the edge of the balcony, but the hometown's sights were best left behind. Everyone had resented her tiny existence, *except your step mother, who doesn't want you anyway. She knows you'll never amount to anything.*

    The humid Floridian breeze buffeted against her face. She brought both arms in, holding the phone against herself while allowing the One Within to present himself. "Maybe there's someone out there who might want to see me right now," she said, leaning against the railing.

    There's literally no one down there who cares about you though, he responded, manipulating himself into a considerable whisper.

    She nodded, blinking both eyes and reaching over the steel barrier supporting her last dregs of life.

    But there may be something for you once you get to the bottom.

    "That sounds all right to me," she whispered with all emotional sensation receding. She had become empty within, insensitive to the incentive that someone as caring as Emily could exist below. "Bitter, sweet, death... It's ... all a dream."

    Dreams can become reality with determination.

    Xandria pulled herself over the railing, holding her phone in plain view. One hand grasping the iron bar behind was everything keeping her afloat: the other retained her only physical record of what made life worthwhile in the past.

    She was startled by a stark whisper at the side: "Time to let it all go."

Her body jolted, fumbling the device out of reach. It began the plunge over two hundred feet, diminishing into an uncertain point amidst the darkness.

Already forgot why you came here?

"You bastard," she snarled through gritted teeth. The light vanished: meeting the same fate as her best friend was pure destiny. He very well recognized her wish, transmitting courage throughout the surrounding blood vessels. *This is what you've wanted for two years now, to end up in the same place where she is.*

"That was all I had left," she whimpered, succumbing to his directive and gifting her emptiness to his desire.

That's more like it now.

The teen nodded to herself, considering all deciding factors: that her disappearance would go disregarded by everyone below, and that every attempt to mend with those around resulted in rejection. "They look at me like I'm some sort of freak," she asserted.

They just don't know what it's like to be trapped like this.

"To feel out of place, like you have no purpose to exist."

Like you can't escape from what's keeping you trapped inside.

"And to be pushed aside whenever you put some effort towards those same people."

Just like that, the voice inside went silent. She enjoyed the final moment to herself, allowing the One Within to have that same luxury. They were finally at peace with one another, sharing the same anticipation of what lay below. Inviting or otherwise, reaching the bottom was their key to acceptance.

She shut both eyes and released every muscle. The hot night air pushed back her body and face, replacing the sensation of letting go with eternal acceleration. Unpersuasive fear took her over past the point of no return, solidifying time within the surrounding pull of gravity.

We are one and this is what we wanted.

Her subconscious agreed. The field rushed up to them, encapsulating her within nothing aside from eternal darkness.

Translation

What is this place?

...

Am I even ... what happened?

Why can't I feel anything?

...

I feel alone inside, like there is no one else in here.

...

Anyone? ... Anyone there?

...

Where did you go?

...

Answer me.

...

Come on, please respond. I can't be without you.

...

Get this light out of my face, and come back.

...

Please...

It's freezing in here, and damp.

I could also rest, since it's pretty relaxing for some reason.

That's it, I've finally got the chance to lay in peace.

Asylum

She managed to pry apart both burning eyes despite the agonizing hammering against the confines of her skull. Resting motionless upon cold damp stone: cold iron pinned down her sore wrists and ankles. She tugged both arms up, halted by the sharp jangle of thick chain and sharp sting from the limbs. The surroundings were incomprehensible, consisting of deceit blackness painted by the sparse reflection of flame dancing on stone. Her heavy body remained far too sore to manipulate, expelling a subtle groan when she forced herself back down.

Panic set in without indication of her whereabouts or how she got there, fueled by an absent mind which lacked stimuli. Twisting her body transmitted chills of nauseating weakness within while attempting to compile the succeeding events replaying behind her eyes. Breathing was nearly impossible, and the musty refreshment brought enough reprieve to blink away some haze, yet her environment remained empty amidst a standstill of time.

She was trapped: the anticipation that someone was waiting to free her drove the pondering of every possibility. "What happened...?" She whispered to herself, triggering an indecisive memory of enslavement. Her breathing leveled out as she made sense of the location: the occasional drop of water on the side combined with prevalent heat and a lack of outwards visibility portrayed the location as a cell or cavern. "Looks like a cave to me," she muttered, remaining unsure against the disconnected thought that undesirable choices leading to prosecution had been made.

A faint speckle of flame in the distance grabbed her vision: the same one casting outwards from within a connecting passage. It resembled an exit, until a muffled gasp reflected off the left side. Her body froze with inexplicable terror, sinking alongside every absurd recognizable breath. It grew louder, transferring the dark memory of a moment brimming with comforting uncertainty and terror. *What's that?* She questioned inside, receiving an abnormal lack of response. She remained still as last resort, forcing her wrists into the same iron that held them.

The noise from the corner strengthened with every one of its breaths: her body shivered alongside each one, heightening perception without direction. Disconcerting scratching scraped an ear, concluded with a tiny grunt and growl. The sounds were frightening yet unreadable, but as before they carried a subtle though profound recognition. The disoriented teen stuck her head towards the left, facing an eerie crimson orb adjoined with an identical white one casting their diluted aura upon the overhanging stone. She withheld a gasp, pressing her back flush against the cavern floor and detecting the memory that someone had always been there no matter what. Her hand reached towards the right pocket by reflex, snagging the chain. Muttering a cure, her own breath choked her as the rattled chain raised alarm.

Her body fell dead silent. Despite the effort, she was unable to hinder the pounding chest and heavy breaths. Several moments passed in attempted silence, hindered by omnipresent fear and occasional shifting from the side.

Her face remained glued to the humid ceiling, barring all stimulus from outside. Her efforts were fruitless, being interrupted by a small torturous whisper: "You're really bad at hiding."

The voice presented immediate recognition, stitching together with its appearance inside the folds of her mind. Regardless, she continued pressing her body into the stone to continue her inanimate endeavor.

"I bet someone's confused," the same whisper added, audibly coming closer and displacing an internal emptiness: "What do you want?!" She shouted, immediately clamping her mouth shut to prevent further instigation. She ignored the queasiness within, finding strength to turn over after having been discovered. The creature conveyed no distinct name, but it was not frightening whatsoever as it floated near her side despite its unworldly appearance. The previous fear within had seemingly vanished despite the vulnerability of being chained to the floor. The black form held one comforting quality about it: company. She had no courage to speak, but the recognition alongside its lack of advancement in an aggressive manner made her wish for it to remain.

The thing drew near, lowering itself at her side. Its quiet voice explained with forced softness, "I want you to know that we did what we had to do."

She cast him a despondent gaze, tangling her dark eyes with the pair set atop impeccable black.

Dropping himself to her eyes, he whispered, "You don't remember me?"

She had no reaction. They stared blank at one another, trying to make sense of everything going on. The girl experienced complete emptiness alongside a scattered mindset: the creature trying to communicate with her held no particular shape below the waist: above, his shape appeared human though narrower with a large disproportionate head topped by a pair of familiar horns. His body tapered down to a black flame whipping around mere inches from the floor, and he seemed to know everything: "You jumped."

Everything within flashed by: rushing through the field, the scary voices, the collision, "You..." She glared, widening both eyes.

"Finally remembered it, I see," the thing sneered, whipping around to her feet and revealing a sickening row of white points making up his mouth.

She froze to the floor: chained to the floor with no escape, the creature before her intertwined with a stark memory of being torn apart from within. "Charlie!" She screamed with everything, recalling that he was the one driving her to ending everything.

"Welcome to hell!" He shrieked, forcing her to scamper back only to be caught. "Leave me alone!" She screamed, shutting both eyes and pulling the iron with all her strength.

"If only it were that simple!" He teased, bringing the inconsistent form above her torso. "You'll never get away from me, Charlie the great! The voice in your head, controlling your deepest darkest desires!"

Her body fell sick, almost unable to contain her guts. She wailed without control, pulling her extremities to the breaking point by the heavy influence of his motive. Terror weighed down her chest, filling her head and forcing hot tears through her eyelids. She feared for her life without the fear of death; "There's no easy way out anymore," he taunted, pressing his face near and widening his persuasive grin.

His jaws snapped at her face, preventing contact by pulling away at the last moment. The girl trapped beneath cried for mercy, unable to fight the one previously kept inside. It may have been another one of his intense manipulations, but the ambience made him out to be very physical. He grabbed her shoulders and pressed them into stone, rattling her frame and pushing the twisted horns towards her eyes. "This time, I really will go through you!"

The notion of being torn apart immobilized her body. "Xandria," he echoed. "I don't like the way you're looking at me." She shut him out again: a horrendous mistake. "Pay attention to me you freak!" The blackened being hollered, "I'll rip out those stupid beady eyes of yours!"

Rasp gasps powered through her effort of self perseverance, influencing Charlie's physical form to retreat. He dashed above her head, making no noise to mask the movement. He flattened his lanky body to the floor. "You can open your eyes now," he whispered, forcing his voice into a comforting hum.

She obeyed through reflex lacking control. He was nowhere to be seen: the voice was the sole indicator of his presence. "Don't do that to me again," she wept, almost unable to speak. She shut her eyes, struggling for breaths. "I've had enough of you ... and you never stop."

A distasteful set of hands pressed her head into stone, blocking a scream: she was being suffocated, jolting in terror and internally begging for mercy without response.

"I don't stop ... because we are one."

No strength remained to fight against her captor.

"Now you better be quiet," he insisted, beginning to release her face from his stringy fingers. "Just don't say anything." He wafted from the floor, returning to her view. "I'll leave you alone for the time being." To his dismay, she nodded, frantically gasping for air.

The sudden click of metal against stone reflected from the walls, shocking the pair and sending Charlie near the conjoined tunnel which cast the noise. Xandria's body tensed up once more with the thought that someone was finally coming to get her. "There's someone coming," he whispered, freezing still in space.

She obliged to his thought, longing for a single unhindered moment of peace. Her body was weak, and her insides felt like liquid. She had no idea where she was, or even what the accompanying one was made of. Held back and hopeless: awaiting the inevitable was the only option.

The deep glow of a transposable flame illuminated the depths, being cast around as if being carried around. Xandria could make out more of Charlie's material shape: despite having been together for years, she never had the chance to see him from afar. He was smaller than herself and rather thin, appearing easy to overpower which initiated the forceful desire to break free.

He glanced back and forth between the girl and cave, disregarding the freshly induced turmoil. Everything remained clearly imprinted on her mind, but the protective reflex did not go unnoticed. A bright flame peered through, casting the shadow of another human being with something eerily spooky about the way it stood, but the thick flame adjacent to it made distinguishing individual features impossible.

The one hovering at her feet dashed behind, placing the girl between the two unknowns. The figure inside the cavern rapidly walked into view with a pair of caped black figures trailing him. He appeared no larger than herself, and about the same age, being followed by a set of bony wings above a thick luxuriant tail appearing the same color as the velvety ears on both sides of his head. Asserting his dominance required no explanation: he rushed past Xandria, shoving the side of his staff into her thigh, imposing a sharp sting. She froze, unable to move with both eyes sinking amidst the fear of her attackers. One of the smaller underlings grabbed her feet with a warm set of bony hands, while the second threw some sort of thick net upon her trapped form. She began screaming, unable to comprehend their attack.

"They won't hurt you, but this one might," the leader called, slamming his metallic device into the wall. The one accompanying her began screaming to no avail: she almost felt bad for him, but the years of torture he had induced upon her were unforgettable.

The two shackles holding her feet back were released, but her energy to revolt was draining fast. Only able to accept those given words: her consciousness began fading, averting all thought to inside. Where was she being taken? There was no conclusion, or answer to where she was. Her eyes began sinking, allowing her one last glimpse at the strange kid: Charlie's neck was trapped within a circle of metal whilst struggling to fight back.

"Don't ... hurt ... him ..." She whispered, fading away too quickly to complete the statement. "He's ... fine as ... me ..."

"This one's going to the old cave, and don't you dare take her anywhere but the good one."

The net was tightened around her body and lifted up, concluding the surrounding with muffled phrases and distant whispers.

Perception lifted into the unknown as her chest fluttered up. Everything faded away, triggering the memory that she had before once faded into nothing...

Hannah:

A *Christmas Murder* is an incomplete fifteen thousand word young adult novella. Cassidy, her mother and her boyfriend don't have a joyful Christmas like they had hoped after Cassidy and her mother are brutally murdered. Cassidy's boyfriend must prove he is innocent.

A Christmas Murder

Cassidy:

One more day till Christmas! I'm so excited! "Cassidy! Cookies are done. Want to help me decorate them?" Mom called from down stairs. She knows how much I love decorating cookies. I hopped down the stairs. I was in a pretty red dress, my brown hair was being held back with a bow. I walked into the kitchen and there were about 29 little Christmas tree cookies sitting on a cookie rack. There was a bowl of green icing set next to them. "Oh good, you're here to help." Mom's bright smile lit up the room.

By the time I finished helping my mom it was nine o'clock at night. "Okay Mom, I'm going to go pick out my outfit for tomorrow then I'm going to get some sleep. Love you!"

She came and gave me a hug "Okay sweetie. Have a great sleep. I'll see you in the morning." She then kissed my forehead. I slowly made my way up the stairs. I walked into my room and headed over to my closet. I was thinking of wearing a dress. Christopher knows I only wear them on special occasions, but he always said I looked gorgeous in dresses. I picked out a black sparkly dress with a sweet heart neckline; it flared out at the bottom with tulle. I've always wanted to wear this dress, but never got the chance.

I slid off the dress I was wearing and slipped on a pair of baggy sweat pants and a black tank top and crawled into bed and headed to sleep.

I wish I could say "visions of sugar plum danced in my head," but they didn't. I wasn't "nestled all snug in my bed," I was tossing and turning all night. I had a bad dream that Christopher was over and my dad got into the house and killed mom, me, then Christopher. It was awful.

It was a beautiful Christmas morning; there was no snow but the sun was shining bright. A light layer of frost covered everything outside. I jumped out of bed. I know, a sixteen year old girl shouldn't really be this excited about Christmas, but I am. I put my brown curly hair into a messy bun and headed down stairs. Christmas is the only time of year I get to see my family and my boyfriend, Christopher is coming down, too. I haven't seen him in almost three months. Not all my family will be there. I have never met my dad. I've only seen pictures. Mom says he's not to be trusted and he's a little messed up in the head. She said that he threatened to kill her when she didn't do something the way he liked it done. She finally had enough of it, so she divorced him. I was really little when it happened only one or two.

I slipped on my white bunny slippers and thumped down the stairs. My baggy sweat pants and black tank top did me no justice. I headed straight to the kitchen, because mom usually makes me pancakes shaped like little Christmas trees on Christmas morning.

"Merry Christmas!" I yelled as I walked into the kitchen. My eyes were drawn to the sink which was where my mom's head was. Her head was floating in the dish water; there were puddles of blood on the counter, spilling onto the floor. I walked a little closer. "M-mom..." I whispered and gently nudged her in hopes that this might be a nightmare.

She fell to the floor. A huge gash was in her throat. Her eyes were shut and her blond hair was slowly turning red from the blood that was getting on it. My vision became blurry.

I covered my hand over my mouth so I wouldn't scream

"Oh god, no!" I couldn't believe what was happening. This all had to be one big bad dream. This couldn't be real. Things like this couldn't happen to me. They just couldn't.

What do I do? Do I call the cops? Do I wait until everyone starts coming over? Do I just hide in my room and pretend like this is all one big dream? Do- Just then I heard the front door creak open;

I always hated the creak of the front door. It's always been like that. The creak reminded me of the time Christopher took me to the fair for the first time,

It was the first time I've ever been to the fair he brought me there for my fifteenth birthday. We were walking around. I held the big pink fluffy unicorn Christopher had won for me from the balloon dart game. Yes I know it was a pointless game that takes little no effort, but this fricken unicorn is so cute.

"Come on." Christopher grabbed my hand and led me through the crowd of people. This was all so new to me. "Step right up folks!"

"Pop the balloon win a prize!"

"DING DING DING WINNER!"

I loved it all so much.

We stopped I front of a big green metal contraption. It was spinning wildly. It looked fun, but every so often I would hear a squeak and a creak coming from it. "Christopher I refuse to go one that spinning metal death trap!" There was no way in hell I was going on that thing.

"Come on Cassidy it'll be fun."

"Fun?! What if I die?!!" Okay maybe I was being a little over dramatic, but it still didn't seem very safe.

"Okay fine, be a party pooper I'll go on it by myself." He ran to get in line. I let out a big sigh and ran after him.

We were next in line. I'm not going to lie. I'm nervous as heck. What if it breaks and I get hurt? All the people that were previously on it stumbled off laughing.

"Next!"

"Come on you'll be fine." Christopher pulled me on to it.

"C-Cassidy? I haven't seen you in so long. Look how much you've grown!" I heard a deep man's voice. I slowly turned around and there was a tall man with brown hair and piercing blue eyes; he also had a big knife in his hand which happened to be covered in blood. He looked extremely familiar.

"D-dad?"

He took a big step closer and pulled me into a hug. I pushed him off me and he stumbled back a little bit. The bloody knife was dropped to the floor; little splatters of blood flew onto our white tiled floor.

"What the hell do you think you're doing?!" I had so many emotions going on I felt like my chest was caving in

"What do you mean, Cassidy? I'm back in your life now. We've got so much to catch up on." He took a few small steps closer.

I turned around and sprinted to the backdoor. "This can't be happening!" That's all that was running through my head.

I made it to the back door. I whipped it open. It's times like these I like living in California. We get close to no snow. I ran out. I looked back to see if my dad was chasing me when I bumped into someone. I fell to the ground. I looked up and it was Christopher my boyfriend.

"Cassidy, why are you outside in your pjs?"

"Christopher I'm so glad to see you!" I jumped up and gave him a quick kiss. "We have to get the hell out of here." I heard a big bang and I was on the ground. I was having difficulties breathing. I was blacking out. I was seeing memories of Christopher and me.

When we first got together, I was late for class because of him; he thought it was a good idea to get coffee before school which sounded like a good idea till he spit his coffee all over me so I had to get changed. I had to stop at my locker, so he stopped and waited for me . I put my hair in a high pony and dusted off my black shirt with swirls and shapes on it. It flared out at the bottom. It complimented my black skinny jeans well. I turned and looked at him "you better have a good excuse as to why we're BOTH late. He pushed me against one of the lockers and kissed me.

When we went hiking together, the view was gorgeous.

When I first met his parents, his mom loved me and so did his dad. When my mom first met him she said he was the nicest boy that I've ever gone out with.

When we went to the beach last summer and got ice cream afterwards.

When he took me to my first party and like a stupid fifteen year old I drank way too much, but he being him, he brought me back to his house and took care of me the next day.

When I broke my arm long-boarding. No story to that one. I just broke my arm and he happened to be with me.

He would always say that his friends found me hot and that they were jealous. My friends were always jealous of our relationship.

Whenever I was sad he could always find a way to cheer me up. The simple things, those are the things I'm going to miss.

He was, no, he IS the best boyfriend anyone could ask for.

He was the only thing I could think of right now, not the fact that my mom just died or that my own father just shot me. In my mind, Christopher was everything. We've been together for almost three years; next month would have been our three year anniversary.

I felt Christopher grab my hands. I started to cry more than all I already was. My cheeks were soaked and I started to taste blood. I couldn't feel my legs or my feet. I was in excruciating pain. I know I was dying. Yes, I accept it. I just don't want to leave Christopher. He's my everything. I slowly opened my eyes. I saw Christopher crying and shaking a little bit.

"Kiss it all better Christopher, please?" My voice was low and raspy. "I'm not ready to go. It's not your fault, love, you didn't know, please never forget about me, I'll be waiting for the day I get to see you again." He started to cry more. I weakly lifted my hand to his face and wiped away his tears as best as I could. His brown eyes were red. I always hated seeing him cry. He doesn't deserve to cry over me...

"I love you," I whispered.

"I love you, too, Cassidy."

He kissed my forehead. I closed my eyes and pulled one of my hands away from his and ran my hand over my stomach and chest trying to find where I was shot. When I felt the hole, it was where my heart is... and in that moment of silence I felt my heart stop.

Christopher:

Her hands are so cold. She was so lifeless which was odd. I've never seen her so still before. I didn't like it. She always used to be so bubbly and full of life. She would live her life to the fullest every single day. Was there something I could have done to prevent this? What if I had shown up earlier? She could have come and lived with me. She told me that her dad was crazy; I just assumed that he wouldn't come back.

I felt the anger filling up inside of me. How could he do this? How could I let this happen?!

There was something different in me right now...I've never felt this angry.

I got up slowly and turned to look at him. He just stood there with an evil grin. In his right hand he held a 9mm hand gun. I stood there for a good five seconds just staring at him, and then I charged at him. I landed on top of him.

He fell to the ground and the gun went flying. I started punching his face repeatedly. He threw a few punches at me as well.

I could easily tell the blood on my hands and my clothes were from him. I was on top of him punching him for a good twenty minutes. I slowly stood up. My hands felt numb and they were shaking. I walked slowly over to the gun and walked back over to the bruised man lying on the ground. I stood over him, the gun pointed down at him. I waited a second and pulled the trigger.

I slowly pulled my phone out and turned it on. A picture of Cassidy and I kissing appeared on the screen. I felt tears start to fall down my cheeks they tickled a little bit, but nothing could make me smile right now.

I punched in 911 and held the phone up to my ear.

"Hello 911. How I may help you?"

I was silent for a few seconds. "My girlfriend has been murdered..."

The phone was quiet. "By whom?"

I'm not going to lie; I felt like a piece of me was killed with her. "Her father..."

"Okay, Hun. I have your location. The police are on their way. I'm going to need you to stay on the phone with me untill they get there okay?"

I just stood there. "Okay." My phone screen went black. My phone must have died. Oh well. They're on their way. I held the phone up to my face and looked myself in the eyes. "You just killed a man..." I whispered to myself, I then saw something move in the corner of the phone screen. I looked a little closer and it looked like Cassidy. I dropped my phone and turned around and Cassidy was standing there , bu, there was still her lifeless body on the ground. She just stood there with her arms heled open. I closed my eyes and shook my head. "You're not really here. You're dead! When I open my eyes, you're going to be gone!" I slowly opened my eyes and she was gone, but the lifeless body lying on the ground was still there. There was a part of me that still wanted

"Cassidy's ghost" to still be there. I slowly walked back over to Cassidy she was just lying there curled up into a ball; I sat down and pulled her limp body onto my lap. I just sat there hugging her lifeless body close to mine. Her face was pale and she was cold, yet her beauty is so unreal her smile was the sun, but now it's all gone.

The police were here in a matter of minutes.

I could hear the sirens in the front yard. I could hear faint voices; I felt my whole world was collapsing. What am I going to do without her? She was my everything. I know that's extremely cliché for a seventeen year old boy to say, but I really did love her and she loved me. He had no right to do that to her. I loved her so god damn much.

I felt a tap on my shoulder. "Son... We're going to need you to come with us." I gently set Cassidy back down onto the ground. I slowly got up and walked out to the front. "Hands behind your back." I looked at them. They violently put my hands behind my back and cuffed them.

"What the hell do you think you're doing?!"

"You're going to prison for first degree murder." They then pushed me into the car.

"I didn't do anything!" I kept repeating myself over and over again but they wouldn't listen to me.

Do they really think I killed Cassidy and her father and her mother! Well I mean, I did kill her father, but not purposely. There was just so much anger and rage built up inside me. I had to get it out. I bet if I hadn't killed him, he would have killed me.

In less than twenty minutes we were at the police station. I was horrified I know what first degree murder means; I could get a death sentence or life in prison, which should be classified as a death sentence.

They got me out of the car there was a bunch of cameras flashing. Ppeople asking questions and saying extremely rude and not true comments: "Why'd you kill your own girlfriend?!"

"Why did you kill her family?!"

"You monster!"

"He should get life in prison!"

They got me inside the police station and put me in a small room. Nothing on the walls, just a table and two chairs. They sat me down and cuffed my hands and feet to the chair. I bowed my head in shame. Yes I felt bad about killing someone, but at least I didn't kill him on purpose... I don't think I killed him on purpose. I heard the door click open. My head shot up. There were two police officers ,one slightly short and chubby and a really tall thin one. The short one sat down in the chair while the tall one stood beside him.

"I'm Officer Jones and that's Officer Joseph and we're just going to ask you some simple questions, okay?"

I slowly nodded my head.

"Okay good, now can you explain what you did today?"

My breathing was shaky. "I woke up this morning at 5:30 to catch my flight from Canada to California. I landed in Long Beach at 9:00am this morning I then got a taxi to Cassidy's. We drove for an hour to get there."

"Okay, so why did you head around the back? Did you know someone was in the house? Were you helping Adam kill Cassidy and his ex-wife?"

"Well, if you had let me finish, I would have told you that I wanted to surprise Cassidy, because she thought I was coming later that night. I went through to front door first and I then saw Amy, Cassidy's mother lying on the floor with a gash in her throat. I ran upstairs to see if Cassidy was in her room. She wasn't. I just wanted more time with her. I never thought any of this would happen." There was a moment of silence before I continued "I was walking around the back when I ran into Cassidy and that's when her father shot her, and that's when I killed him..."

"So you admit you killed Cassidy's father?" Officer Jones said resting his arms on the table and raising one of his bushy eyebrows.

" That I will admit, but I would never do anything to harm Cassidy or her mother."

Officer Jones looked up at Officer Joseph and nodded his head. Officer Joseph left the room. "How did you kill Adam?"

I leaned forward on the table so I was closer to him. I let out a small sigh. "After he shot Cassidy, I got extremely mad and lunged at him. I then punched him in the face. He fought back, but it wasn't enough. I then got up and grabbed his gun and shot him." I then fell backwards and hit the back of my chair with my back. "If I wouldn't have done what I did, there was a good chance that he would have shot me, too."

Officer Jones nodded his head and left the room I was sat there for a while in silence left alone with my thoughts, I closed my eyes and started to cry; I hate crying for me I find it a sign of weakness.

"Please stop crying, dear, you don't deserve to cry even over me," a soft sweet voice whispered in my ear.

"Cassidy." My eyes shot open, but there was no one in the room.

Just then the door opened again and there stood Officer Jones. He walked over to me. "I feel bad for you kid. You seem nice. You shouldn't have to go to jail; you're too young." He uncuffed my hands and feet then brought me out of the room and got me back into the police car.

"Where are we going?"

Officer Jones looked back in his mirror so he could look at me. "You're going to jail. I'm sorry."

Tears started to fall down my face. I think I was more stressed out than anything.

We drove for a good hour before we reached our destination which was, of course, jail. I got out of the car and Officer Jones came over and escorted me into the jail

"Christopher McNeal, you're going to be staying here for a long time." I glared at the lady at the front. I got handed an orange jump suit, shoes and bedding and was taken to a small bathroom with no windows just a toilet, a mirror and a sink. "You can change in here."

I nodded my head slowly and walked in and closed the door. I slid off the clothes I was wearing and put on the orange jump suit and the white shoes, which were really uncomfortable. I looked in the mirror and a couple tears fell down my face. "I miss her so much," I quietly whispered to myself. I came back out and handed the guard my clothes. I was then shown my cell room. I didn't, however, get a roommate, which I was thankful for. The guard pushed me into the cell. "See you bright and early the next morning." He closed the door covered in bars.

There was a small bed a toilet a mirror and a sink; I set the blankets, sheets and the one pillow I was given onto the bed. I sat down on the bed and started to cry. All I have is a memory. All it is a memory. I lay on the un-made bed and stared at the ceiling. "Christopher..." I heard a faint whisper. I sat up and looked around the room, but I saw no one. From my bed, I looked in the mirror and I saw Cassidy standing in her baggy sweat pants and her tank top. "It's not your fault, love, you didn't know." At this point I didn't know what was real and what wasn't. "I love you." I whispered to her. "Bye, Christopher. I'll see you soon." She then disappeared.

I started to cry more. *This can't be happening.* I lay back down onto bed and hugged a pillow. "Stay with me till I fall asleep, please?"

Andrew:

The Arise is an incomplete fantasy novella. When Brandon is faced with a zombie apocalypse, he must get himself and his family to the safety of his uncle's cabin.

Note: language and violence warning

The Arise

It was a cool day in September although the moon was out and there were no clouds in the sky. All I remember is being up at 4:30 in the morning walking down the stairs in my purple onesie, to my surprise the TV had been left on. As I went to turn it off breaking news report said, "The bodies of the dead are rising." I run to the window and see a bunch of people walking around outside dragging limbs.

I thought to myself I need to phone my friends. First I phone Tyrone (old friend from military) and tell him what's happening "Dafuq you talking about dude?"

"I mean the enemy is attacking."

"How?"

"Don't know but we're going right now and bring the tanker we'll need it."

"Okay."

"Sam we need to go now!"

"What the f! Brandon, it's 4:50!"

"Get up now or we are going to die!!"

"What?"

"Just look outside."

"WHAT ARE THOSE!!!!!?"

"They're the undead. I'm going to get the guns and ammo you pack food and medicine."

"Okay, I'll get right on it."

"Hey T you there?"

"Yah why?"

"Because it has happened."

"What happened?"

"The Panamas have attacked. Do you have your med kit?"

"Always."

"Good. Let's go."

Sam and I load my truck up to the canopy with food and med's for about 3 months each when we all get to the edge of town I notice something weird up ahead "Everyone stop, road block up ahead."

The convoy of truck comes to a halt in front of the blockade. "What is the meaning of this? If you do not get out of our way I will make a way!"

"Sir please head back to your house without delay."

Good thing I installed this bumper "Sam hold on to something." (runs through the blockade) "Tyrone you got that tanker."

"Yah and its right full of gas."

"Sweet."

"Where to now, Brandon?" asked Sam.

"Uncle Brian's cabin."

About fifteen minutes later Sam notices something in a ditch. "Hey isn't that Greg's truck?"

"Yah I think so, hey guys stop for a sec."

"Why are we stopping?"

"Raiding that wreck."

"Oh ok."

"Hey, Greg. You all right?"

"What's it to you?"

"Dude. We're trying to help you out here."

"F off I don't need your help military man."

"You maggot you are not allowed to call me that."

"OW!" yells Tyrone.

"What happened?" yelled Brandon.

"I think I cut myself."

"Shit, everyone back into the trucks!" As we were driving I notice that my truck is running on empty. "Hey guys see that gas station up ahead?"

"I do," said Tyrone.

"I need to make a quick stop there, if that's ok."

"Sure". As we pulled into the pumps I saw someone walking around inside the station "Hey Sam, hand me that pistol in the back seat."

"Why?"

"Just do it."

"Ok...?"

After Sam hands me the gun I take aim at his hand. *If he doesn't flinch I aim for his head if he does we go and help him.* Bang, He didn't flinch! "Sam hand me the shotgun". BANG.

"Brandon, I think it's dead."

"Yep, do you want to grab some stuff?"

"Sure."

While they were grabbing stuff, Tyrone and I were filling up the trucks with gas. "Hey Brandon, you might want to come see this."

"Why?"

"Just come here."

"Sweet, another gas tanker."

"Hey Brandon" yelled Tyrone.

"What?"

"It's getting dark, should we stay the night here?"

"It's not getting dark, those are rain clouds."

"Are you sure? Because they don't look like it."

"Sam, come here."

"Yeah?"

"Do you know how to drive?"

"Yeah, why?"

"Because I need you to drive my... What's that sound? Greg what are you doing here?"

"I hopped in the back when we left my truck."

"How much have you eaten?" Brandon sighed.

"Only one small bag of salt and vinegar chips."

"Ok then, you'll have to ride with Sam."

"Fine". It was about 7:30 p.m. when we found the dirt road that lead towards Brian's cabin then Sam notices something.

"Hey Brandon, you have a flat tire."

"Where?"

"First two tires on the back passenger side."

"Ok, everyone pull over."

Just as I had grabbed the spare tire out of my truck I swear I heard some sort of growling "Tyrone come put this tire on for me. Greg help out or we will leave you here."

"Where are you going?"

"I'm going to find out what that sound was."

"Ok."

As I was walking into the forest I noticed that there were tracks on the ground. *I've seen these type of tracks before, but where?* All of a sudden I notice something running towards me so I quickly roll out of the way. "What was that?" *It looks like some sort of dog?*

Just a second after Sam calls me "Brandon! We need your help" after I hear that I run back through that forest to see a hundred dead zombies and even more coming, so I grab my katana and go berserker on them, give or take an hour about three hundred zombies were dead and we were back on the now mucky road that lead to Brian's timber cabin "What was that about?"

"Greg blew up the clutch for your truck."

"And why was he driving my truck?" I roared.

"He was trying to leave you behind so you had to deal with the hoard; also he got hungry and ate your bag of carrots and ranch dressing."

"Ok then Greg. I'm sorry but we have to leave you here," I said.

"No you... you can't!" Greg yelled.

"Ok then give me a good reason why we shouldn't leave you here?"

"You... you just can't!"

"LIAR, yes I can."

"Prove it!"

"Hey Sam. What gear is my truck in?"

"I think third, but I'm not sure."

But just as I drive away I hear a loud noise, "What was that!" I yelled.

"Brandon, run! Greg just shot Tyrone!"

"WHAT?!"

"Just run, we will meet you at Brian`s cabin!"

Though it took us awhile to make it to Brian`s but with time comes pain, with the only casualty being one of my best friends, Tyrone. "Bring Greg to me. Now!" A few minutes later Greg walked in "Gregory Joseph Timely, you are being charged with second degree murder, attempted GTA and treason.

Armando

Free is an incomplete historical fantasy novella. Cedric must rescue his people from the despotic King Merek who has stolen his birth right.

Free

The night is dead. As the rain dripped onto my forehead, I looked up at the sky. Stars shone in my eyes. The area felt dead. The guards were asleep. It's a shame that King Merek couldn't hire superior guards that don't idle. I guess we're in luck.

"It's time."

Let me tell you a story about the story of the fallen clan; the resistance clan. It was one an ordinary day at the village. We plotted a plan for escape, planned our assassination of the psychotic king who promised to change the kingdom for the better. Unfortunately this was all a lie. His words all were deceiving, but people followed him. They worshiped him. The people of the kingdom believed in his mendacious words. The resistance clan were the only ones who weren't brainwashed by his nonsense.

The king before was King Arthur, Merek's father. People adored him. He was a proper king. He was passionate and caring. But one night King Arthur was assassinated and Merek took the place of his dad. Ever since the death of his father ,he abused his power, took away everyone's freedom by building a wall around the kingdom so no one was allowed to leave. He told stories of the monsters that were lurking around the woods: sea monsters and other nonsense that the towns people believed in. Let's just say the people who lived in the kingdom didn't even know what was at the other side of the wall. They have never seen a glimpse of reality;

they have never seen actual animals or trees. Merek had other nations to work for him, and whoever got in his way got executed in public.

My dad always told stories about how he and Merek were childhood friends. They did everything together and would visit each other at a daily basis, but Merek was bullied a lot by kids; he was kicked around and harassed. He tried telling them that his dad was the king, but they didn't believe him. My dad wasn't there to back him up, and his dad was never there to show up. His mother was assassinated. Merek had a sad back story. He used to smile. Now he's emotionless, careless. It's a shame that it had to end like this.

That ordinary day wasn't the ordinary at all. That very day I could hear the horses from the bushes and it still haunts me every day and every night. The sound ceased. I thought it was just the horses that we had available for the clan, but it wasn't. It was a horde of gladiators. They wore armor and wielded powerful weapons. I asked myself how they found our village, since the village was hidden away from society.

"Cedric!" My mom screamed nervously.

"Janet, be quiet." My dad whispered.

We were in the small hut. The houses were set on fire; members of the clan were being slaughtered, and this was not a good sight. It was painful to look at. My frown turned into sobs. From the distance I could see a figure who wore a crown. It looked like King Merek. As he got closer to the hut, we knew for sure that it was him, the guilty king who destroyed the village.

"Sir Walter, I know you're hiding in there," he shouted.

"I'll try to negotiate with the king." Dad insisted we stay inside.

"Walter! You're going to die!" My Mom started to panic. "If you're coming out I am, too!"

My dad didn't say a word. I had never been so afraid in my whole life. I've seen that expression before: it was the face of murder and King Merek was craving homicide. My dad opened the door and my mom stood up and walked out with him.

"We surrender, just don't hurt our son!"

I looked out the window. King Merek looked expressionless, as if he didn't feel any remorse or shame of what he annihilated.

"Sir Walter, I don't care if you surrender or not, I just want you killed." He said calmly.

I heard a loud whoosh.

My Mom and Dad were shot down and killed right before my eyes. Tears fell from my eyes.

"Search the building," he insisted.

At this point there was no chance of escape. The Gladiators busted into the hut.

"We found the kid!" One of them shouted.

King Merek entered the room. He eyeballed me and grinned. "I will find a good use of you." He looked amused.

He kicked me down as my vision faded into black. I woke up in a cellar where I was forced to mine.

In the mine I met two of my fellows about the same age as me. Leo and Kaylein. Leo had short red hair and blue eyes. He had been abandoned by his parents. Kaylein had long hair blonde hair that went down to her hips. She had hazel brown eyes and a pale skin. She going to be executed, but Merek needed more miners to build a bigger wall. We had planned an escape for years, and tonight was the night we escape once and for all.

Now let me explain what the plan is: I distract one of the guards and Kaylein will steal the key from the one of the guards, we'll pretend to mine some rocks and wait until midnight where we would be locked up in a cellar from a different guard. We'll use the key to unlock the door and walk out. At midnight the guards should be sleeping in a tent or a hut, we'll sneak into their tents and steal a weapon: a sword, a knife and a spear. Leo will be our navigator and find where the castle is, there is usually a group of mercenaries guarding the doorway, so Leo will make a diversion and distract them. Kaylein and I will sneak into the castle. Tthere will be a room with the keys and the key to the gate should be there. We'll meet up with Leo and open the gate to freedom. We are passionate that this plan will work. We have been studying for years. If we fail, at least we'll die trying.

"Leo and Kaylein, search for weapons, and be careful."

I tiptoed into one of the huts and scanned the area for weapons. At the far corner there was a knife, probably used for cooking, but it's good enough. I quietly picked it up and walked out. As I walked out Kaylein and Leo each had found a weapon: Leo had a spear and Kaylein had a sword. I felt kind of embarrassed just a little tiny knife, but it would do for now.

"Leo, you know the way to the to the castle right?"

Leo delivered food around the kingdom so he was quite fast on his feet and worked better by himself, so I let him lead the way.

"We need to walk north and take an east turn and there should be a castle"

"How do you even know where the castle is?"

"When my parents abandoned me the king used me as a delivery man until I was sixteen. When years later he didn't need me anymore, he enslaved me." he whispered.

We proceeded to walk north and I looked around. The place was trashed. We saw all sorts of disturbing things, like torture devices. There seemed to be no guards around here so we knew we were safe, but the area smelled so bad. I saw a bucket that was surrounded by flies. My curiosity got the best of me so I checked. I was shocked of what I saw; it was a person's head. It looked like one of the slaves had been decapitated. I vomited onto the ground.

"What's wrong, Cedric?" Kaylein whispered in a soft voice.

"Oh god!" She was also petrified by what she saw.. She looked disoriented.

"That is what happens to slaves if they don't listen to orders. They are executed and their bodies are left to rot." It sounded like Leo has seen this happen before.

Leo insisted that we get out of this area as soon as possible, which was probably a good idea. We proceeded to walk. The area after that was completely normal, just a place full of huts, campfires, and tents. After a walk that seemed like forever, we took the east turn and from the distance we could see the castle.

That was only the beginning. There were mercenary guards protecting the doorway. We hid behind a bush away from view and sat down with our backs against a tree.

"What are we going to do now?" Kaylein asked.

"You guys keep hiding in the bush, and I will make a diversion and distract the guards, and once they have my attention you guys make your move and get into the castle." Leo sounded so calm, I didn't want to say a word, I'm sure he will lose them.

"Where are we going to meet you?" Kaylein scratched her head in confusion.

He pointed at the tree near the gate.

"I will be hiding up in that tree." He smiled.

I smiled back. "Sounds like a plan." Leo was a smart person. I was sure he would make it out alive.

He stood up and created a diversion, which caught the mercenary guards' attention. The plan was working as planned so far. We slowly ran towards the castle and opened up the door. We thought the place would be filled with guards, but I guess we are in luck again. The castle was beautiful: a shiny marbled floor, statues, gargoyles and they even water fountains. I looked up at the chandelier and it was brighter than a star. There was a stair case that went up to the second floor. Leo said that the key room was around here somewhere.

"Kaylein, check the doors at your left and I'll check the right."

"All righty."

I proceeded to the right and checked every room; there were about four bedrooms and two washrooms, so it must have been at the left. Kaylein was showing me sign languages, so I walked towards her and I was right. There was the key room. I had my fingers crossed hoping that the door wasn't locked. I slowly placed my hands on door knob. I twisted it and heard it click. It was opened. My heart started to pound knowing that we were close from freedom. We entered the room and there was an endless number of keys. The keys to every room was in here. Kaylein looked around for signs that had gate labeled on it, and I did the same thing.

After countless minutes of searching I heard a loud scream from a distance. It sounded like Kaylein, I rushed and searched for where that sound came from. There was a human figure I know that there was something wrong, Merek wouldn't leave the door opened especially if it was the ticket to freedom. I was right: it was Merek, and behind him were the keys for the gate. He held Kaylein against her will with the blade almost touching her throat.

"Look who finally showed up?" he grinned.

"Let her go, I'm the one you want."

I was facing the man who had destroyed my village and killed my family. I didn't show any fear, just anger and hatred. Watching Kaylien suffer reminded me of the people of our village.

"Let her go!" I shouted.

He pushed Kaylein off to the side. I pulled out my knife, and the grin on this face turned into a laugh.

"You think you can kill me with that kitchen knife? It's okay, kiddo. You will join your clan soon."

"I will go easy on you." He kicked Kaylein's sword towards me. "Now let's have a real fight shall we?"

He charged at me knocking the shelf from behind me. I step away and parried his slash.

"Take the keys now! Kaylein!" I shouted as loud as I could.

She jolted back up and snatched the key from the shelf.

"Grrrr. That stupid woman!" Merek ran at full speed leaving him opened but he was almost at Kaylein so I jumped him, forcing him onto the ground.

"GO, Kaylein! I will be fine, I promise!"

"I can't just leave you here!" she yelled as tears went down her cheeks.

"Just go! I promise I'll be back!" She took an exit and ran for her dear life.

Merek jabbed at the stomach; and stood back up on his feet. I tumbled back. We were both on our feet.

"How did you know we were going to make a move tonight?"

He smiled. "I ordered the guards to sleep. It was all part of the plan, young man."

"And as soon as the guard told me about the missing key; I made my move."

I knew something was wrong; he wouldn't let us out without a fight. "You really are one hell of a king." I sighed.

"I've surpassed my father. He was a terrible king."

I hoped he was joking around; just hearing him say it made me want to cringe. "A great king? You're a king who decided to fill our minds with lies and the next thing we see is people treating us like we have committed crime! Now our clan is non existent because of you."

"Your clan caused too much trouble. It needed to be destroyed."

Every word he said made me furious. His face was expressionless; he felt absolutely no remorse of what he did.

"You really are thick in the head!"

"Your father died for nothing huh?!"

"I killed my father," he smiled.

I tried to swallow but my mouth was too dry. Merek was a psychopath all right.

"Of course, I wouldn't be telling you this if I was going to let you leave." He stepped closer.

He was expectedly strong and managed to tackle me, knocking me back on the ground. The blades came deathly close. His abdomen was opened and I stabbed him again, as he screamed in agony. I pushed him away from me as he started to cough up blood. I could hear footsteps coming from the hallway. This felt like déjà vu. It sounded like the horses from that very day.

The door burst open. I looked down on my bloody hands and felt disoriented. The mercenary guards pointed their swords at me. "Sir, two of slaves have escaped." He looked over to Merek. He looked frightened; and acted hostile towards me.

I smiled. I was happy that they made it out, even though I lied to Kaylein. Shame on me. I leaned towards Merek and whispered into his ear, "I'll see you in hell."

After the death of King Merek the kingdom changed dramatically. One of the mercenary guards who killed Cedric was now the new king. He was the best king the kingdom has had in years. He had a dream to see the other side of the wall, so he wanted to work for King Merek in hopes of at least seeing a glimpse of the other side. Once he held the crown, he could change the kingdom for the better. He banned slavery and ordered workers to bust a hole into the wall. People spent their time outside the wall, travelling, searching for new lands , while kids played. Some may still be petrified of the monster that lurked in the woods, and sea monsters. The new king told them that it was all fake. The king's name was King Meliodas and he is the first king to ever change Kingdom from prison to freedom. As for Leo and Kaylein, they found a home they belonged to. They found a family that cared for them. They accepted the fact that Cedric was dead, and every day they would thank him for his sacrifice. It was that one day that Leo and Kaylein visited the kingdom to talk to the king.

Leo knocked on the castle door; the door was opened by a butler.

"Who are you two young fellows?" he smiled.

"I would like to see the king." Leo asked.

"Right this way, sir." They were both surprised at the change.

The butler escorted them to the kings throne, where the king looked at Leo. He looked confused because Leo looked familiar. "Do I know you?" Meliodas asked while stroking his beard.

"We were the kids who escaped that night."

He looked at Leo, with a frown. The guards were pointed their spears towards them.

"We just want to talk." Kaylein insisted.

"Do you know a boy named Cedric by any chance?" Leo looked at him with a serious expression.

"He was the boy I killed."

Leo and Kaylein started to shed tears.

"He was a bad guy. He needed to be killed."

"He wasn't a bad guy, not even close." Leo smiled. "Let me tell you a story about a boy who saved the kingdom."

"Let him speak."

The guards put down their weapon.

The king was willing to hear them out. Leo and Kaylein explained what happened that night. The king had the same dreams as Cedric did. They both wanted a glimpse of reality. The king regretted his actions and started to shed tears. "I'm sorry! I really am!"

Leo and Kaylein smiled. "How about we treasure his sacrifice?" Leo placed his hand on this shoulder.

"It's okay; if he was here he would tell you to follow your dreams and let others have freedom they deserve."

Meliodas wiped his tears and agreed. Leo and Kayleen left the kingdom and a month later, a statue of Cedric was built in the middle of the kingdom.

"Thank you Cedric."

Celeste:

Six Months is an incomplete ten thousand word young adult verse novella. Elise Mackenzie had a simple life living in a small town going to an even smaller school, getting to see the boy of her dreams once every week. But her cozy little life gets torn apart when a doctor tells her she has incurable leukemia. She has six months left to live. Time is of the essence; this is her chance to live like there do no tomorrow.

Six Months

You know that moment
When your chest is too tight
Your lungs are collapsing
You're losing your fight
So desperately searching
For any escape
Anything is better than this
They're staring at me
My secret is out
Before I had a chance to run
To hide what he found out about
It was supposed to be a secret
But somebody leaked it
So now I'm here
All eyes on me
Trying desperately to disappear
Right now
I just want to leave
I don't know what I'm more afraid of
Seeing you again
Or never seeing you again
What if I come just one last time?
Will there be fresh humiliation infecting my wounds
Will you hate me for bringing attention to you?
What if I see you?

Will you look my way?

Will you even bother?

Will you have something to say?

But what if I stay home

Will you notice I'm gone?

Will you miss me or will you even care

Will you wonder

Where did she go? She was here last time

Blending into the snow

So what if I don't go what if I stay home

What if you don't miss me and I stay all alone

What if you love me?

What if you don't?

What if this time I break

Like an old china doll?

Should I sit this one out

Or will you catch my fall?

Counting down the minutes

Till I see you again

I've made my decision

Sealed my fate

Started my future

But I still have to wait

Every second is brutal

Every minute hurts

An hour might kill me

But seeing you might be worse

There's no way of knowing

Just what you will do

Will you catch me with open arms

Or will I hit empty air

And fall?

I saw you today

I missed you so much

Before this I was terrified

Now all I want is your touch

I saw your bright shining smile

The crinkles by your eyes

I haven't seen that in a while

But then I realized

That smile wasn't for me

I can't just win your love

But still I sit and hope

That's all it will take

Is a prayer to above

Lying in my soft warm bed

All tucked in

Covers pulled up to my ears

Trying hard to forget my scars

The new ones and the old

Trying to forget my emptiness

From stories that will never be told

My eyes welling up with tears

I remember when I was twelve

Thought I had it all figured out

I thought I knew everything that I knew what life was about

Had my first love, first heartbreak, first blade to hit my skin

At that time I thought that meant everything

Nothing could be worse

But then life hit even harder and I almost ended up in a hearse

I know I'm not the only one

With problems of my own

But it's still a terrible feeling

To feel all alone

Sitting in the hallway

With friends, but so alone

The only thing I want right now

Is to walk around and roam

To visit where you're hiding

To see your fiery hair

And your dark chocolate eyes

Because if I don't

I'll slip further into oblivion

Emptiness is my fate

I hope I can find you

Before it's too late

When life gives you lemons

Make lemonade

Well life misplaced my lemons

Gave them to somebody else

So now I'm just here

Sitting all by myself

Life gave me nothing

Not even a seed

Life gave me an empty pitcher
But that's not at all what I need
Because right now
All I need is
You
Woke up late
The fog of sleep welcoming me back to bed
To my soft warm blanket
Lay my head on a cloud
Sleep my day away
Sleep away my problems
Sleep away my pain
Sleep away the fact that I may never see you again
Slipping in and out of consciousness
I try to wake up I need to fight it
I'm going to fail
As I slip on some clothes I know
Sleep will prevail
Choke down some breakfast and run out the door
Buts I race down the stairs I trip
Tumbling
Crashing
As I hit the ground I know
This isn't my day
The first time I saw you
I knew I was stuck
You are my perfection
From my dreams you've been plucked

I love your dark chocolate eyes
And your cute button nose
From your fiery orange hair
To the tips of your toes
I love the way your eyes crinkle up
Every time that you smile
So why don't you stay here with me
And talk for a while
Your sad blue eyes
Drowning in pain
I wish I could do something
Anything
To make this hurt go away
You've always been with me
My best friend for life
All I can hope right now
Is that you won't lose to your knife
I wish I could tell you
All you want to hear
But instead I sit helpless
Overcome with fear
What if I lose you?
How will I cope?
Would I be able to go on?
Business as usual
Or would I lose out to the rope
I get to see you today
I can't wait

Seconds feel like hours
Minutes like weeks
I memory flashes into my mind
The first time I saw you
When you walked into my world
Speckled with a deep brown and a splash of orange and red
Like a flash of fire
And now I get to see you again
Once a week feels like torture
So much wasted time
I know your full name now
And it sounds too good mixed up with mine
Sweet on the lips
Rolls off the tongue
You are an angel
Heaven here I come
You weren't there
I didn't see you
I guess you don't care
I'm terrified
Over thinking it all
What if you died
What if you gave up
And you stop coming at all
And I'll never see you again
And you don't catch my fall
I miss you already
How will I know?

I'll have to wait till Sunday

Please don't go

I wish that I could reincarnate my childhood

Go back to the days

Of juice pouches

And naps

When my only problems were in math

And who I was friends with didn't matter

I wish I could go back to the time

That playing tag was fun

And nobody was self-conscious

Of how well they could run

And the scale

Was just something you sang with your friends

While you flew to the moon

From the tree in your backyard

And if you got hurt it was okay

Your mom would kiss it all better

So you could go back out

And play

Little Miss Leizel

Oh, she's such a witch

Hungry for power

Getting worse by the hour

She's the world's biggest bitch

Never mind

I shouldn't be saying that

I'm trying to be kind

Trying so hard to be respectful
And silent of course
So I shouldn't think twice
About the no good
Nasty
Leizel von Ice
Power crazy
You think you're so perfect
Just because you're older than me
You're so not worth it
With your snooty little stare
And your icy little glare
Like everyone is underneath you
Just bugs to be crushed under your feet
Always bragging
You think you're the cream of the crop
When really you're not
But nobody really listens
Nobody really cares
Because nobody really likes you
All you do is talk about yourself
About how good you've done
When in reality you haven't
But still you think you're the absolute best
That you're right and everyone else is wrong
It's your way or the highway
So I'll take my chances
On the road

I have a new obsession
He's all that's on my mind
His mischievous smile
Melts my heart
But I know were way to far apart
You'll never ever know me
Like I wish that I knew you
I only see you in the movies
There must be something I can do
Some way for you to see me
A way for us to meet
I wish that you were real
Wouldn't that be sweet?
We could rule the world together
Everyone kneeling at my feet
You could be the king
And I could be your queen
You could jump out of the movies
And come and rule with me
Once upon a time
Life was simple
Sublime
Eating peanut butter sandwiches and pop
Lemon lime
Swimming in my backyard pool
I had a trampoline so I was cool
And when I fell down I just got right back up
And when I ran around it didn't matter

The size of my cup
I could wear short shorts and my shirts were too small
But I didn't care
I was having a ball
Playing chase with my friends
But now they're all gone
Moved away
From this forever shrinking town
But I'm still here
People come and go
And it won't be long till I'm gone to
Out on my out
Still not knowing just what to do
I haven't seen you lately
You haven't been there
I really miss you
Miss your fiery red hair
I used to be hopeful
I couldn't wait for the day when I got to see you
But you never come anymore anyway
Where did you go?
Where are you hiding?
I miss you so much
My sanity's sliding
I've forgotten how you look only a vague outline in my head
If I don't see you soon
I may never see you again
You were my miracle

My wish on a star

But you've lost all your magic

Fizzled out

Someone left the box open

Ajar

I don't know what I would do

If I didn't have you

You are my best friend

My other half

If you're in pain, I'm in agony

If you're happy, I'm overjoyed

I would do anything for you

Except swim in seaweed

That's something I would never do

If you cry I cry

You feel like my brother

Protecting me from this world, shielding me from all the bad things and people

That plan to hurt me

And in turn I also shield you, with your innocent blue eyes

And your shy little smile

People see you as someone to use and abuse

But I'm the only one aloud to do that

Because what are friends for

And you are the best one I've got

Searching

Struggling

Coming up with nothing

But what did I expect
Did I expect him to notice?
Did I expect him to care?
Did I think that he would just see me?
And my world would be repaired
That my scars your disappear
And my pain would go away
That a miracle would happen
And you'd ask me to stay
I don't know what I was thinking
How could this have worked?
I should have gone slower
So no one got hurt
I said so many things that I really regret
But now I'm just left with the emptiness
In my chest
I have a tough decision
Which one do I choose?
The one I've known forever
Or the one who's shiny and new
The one I've known forever
Almost always talks to me
We laugh; we rant, and joke around
As happy as can be
I'm comfortable when I'm with him, to me he feels like home
But he's not always there for me
When I'm all alone
The one who's shiny and new I don't know what to do

If he looks my way I run away

I can't say one word

There is no talking to him

If I try I just freeze up

Whenever he's around me I fly away like a bird

I feel so excited whenever he looks my way

It's too bad I'm so shy and that I don't stay

I can't decide between them

Hook, line and sinker in stuck

If I choose one I will hurt the other

And I'd rather get hit by a truck

You little ankle biter

That's what he always told me

And now he's almost gone

He's 31

On both sides we got the call last night

Grandpa had a stroke

As my mom burst into tears

I sat frozen, helpless

Her poor dad

I still remember when we planted a garden in my backyard

Only planted radishes

His favorite

Spicy little apples

But now he can't eat them

Now he's in pain

He's stopped making jokes

He just waits for his day

Smashing

Aching

All around me the earth is shaking

Screaming

Crying

I feel like I'm dying

My head is burning, shouldering flames

But nothing here can numb my pain

What if my worst fear is coming back to life?

What if my leukemia scare is for real now and I'm going to die

All of those things will never get to do

Never get married, start a family, or drink any booze

My life can't be over it hasn't even begun

If this is really happening it won't be much fun

Slowly dying, never crying

Getting weaker and weaker by the day

All my friends will move on

And my family will mourn

At the loss of little old me

Festering feeding

It's growing inside me

Eating my blood away

Destroying my bones taking me away from my home

I wish it would go away

It's taken control

It's taking its toll and my life is what I must pay

Day by day it's eating away

All my hope and dreams

As the doctors al hover

Telling me I will recover

They tell me in strong and that it won't bring me down

But they're wrong

I feel it spreading

And the day I'm dreading

Gets closer

With every hour

Not much time is left for me

I can't give up can't let them see

I look so bad so pale

I feel so fragile

Way to frail

It seems like just yesterday that everything way good

I had my whole life ahead of me but I never understood

How precariously I perched, dancing on a wire

One wrong move and I fell off

My old life got shattered

I will never get married

Having children is out

Nobody could love me and that I know without a doubt

I'll get one last summer

One last summer love

Till I leave, go above

I'll never get to travel

Never get t roam

The only sights I'll ever see

Will be around my home

Looking back on the day
The doctors took my life away
Took away my hopes and dreams
Took away my everything
Walking in the door that day
Nothing worse could come my way
As they took my blood and told me to wait
Told me I would get the diagnosis soon
In less than a day
As we drive home my mom starts to cry
We know without a doubt that I'm going to die
When we get to the house I go to my room
I open my window to let out this gloom
I phone all my friends
And tell them the news
Six months from now
It's me they're going to lose
I need to stop moping around
I've waited a precious week
Waited time I don't have
I can sleep when I'm underground
For now I will do
All I've ever wanted
Never ending freedom
So my parents won't be haunted
The world is my oyster
My cup of tea
But what's going to happen when they bury me

Six feet underground

They won't hear me scream

They won't hear a sound

What if this is all just a practical joke

To see what I do

If I choose door number one

Or door number two

If I turn to destruction

Or innocent fun

Soon it won't matter

Because I will be done

I met someone today

Who made me feel ok?

Like I wasn't about to die

And I wasn't at all shy

Looking for nothing

I finally found something

Someone

Well, this should be fun

How should I tell him, my future is grim?

I've found my new soul mate, Better write down the date

Twenty-three weeks from now my life will go down

Like the titanic, my once unsinkable ship now has more than one chip

I'm falling apart and I don't want a broken heart

He lives so far away but I might get to see him one day

We both love to read but the story of my life looks bleak

If I could truly meet him for real face to face

To hold his hand and for him to tell me it's ok

Then I think this whole situation
Could just go away
As I walk down the hallway
I think of last night
Talking to him and forgetting my fright
Starting over
Fresh and out of the blue
Out with the old and in with the new
With his talk of adventure
Of flying through the sky
I really want to try it, hopefully before I die
We could soar across the ocean
Dancing with the moon
If I ever want to try it I better try it soon
If I ever have a chance
At a somewhat normal life
I don't think I would take it, wouldn't go under the knife
I couldn't get the surgery
Because it doesn't exist
So I really better finish
All the things that are on my list
Well, this is amazing
A beautiful sight
I'm up so high
It's like I have wings
I'm tired of waiting
I just want to fly
Get it out of the way

Before I have to say goodbye
I'm glad we got up here
Up among the stars
Soon I will be among them
It doesn't seem that far
Seems like I could just lift up my arms
And fly away, away from harm
What a very spectacular sight
I'm so very glad
He took me out tonight
Slashing, crashing
My pain rehashing
Burning, scorching
The world is torching
Crazy, smoldering
A fiery inferno
Will I survive it, how about no
Melting the ice turning water into steam
It hurts so much this better be a dream
It's too much to handle I think I might burst
But to go through it without Levi
Nothing could be worse
He is the freezing
The ice to my fire
He is my cool breeze lifting me higher
Away from the pain and the terrible torture
The waiting is worse in that stupid hospital wheelchair
And all the poking and prodding is giving me bruises

My skin is to week I'm scared I will lose it
One two
I don't know what to do
Three four
Here's two more
Five six
Stones and sticks
My bones are breaking
I'm done with this
I've done nothing wrong; all I did was save a friend
And trust me if I had a chance, I would do it again
I wouldn't do anything different at all
Even though right now I feel so small
All the people who hate me and want me to die
Are getting their wish
And that makes me cry
It won't be long now till they won't have to deal with me
I won't be in the way and that really sucks
That it will make their day
And to all of those people I say a big f--- you
Because I really don't care about anything you do
Going to my uncles funeral
Soon that will be me
Lying cold in the casket as dead as can be
People will come to pay their respect
They will say things like she was gone to soon and she was so young
Such a sweet girl to be taken from this world
They will cry for a while

Then it will be done
I'll be taken to my grave where my body will never see the sun
I will sleep now forever
And people might visit when they feel all alone
And if I'm here I will listen
And if I'm not then I won't
But I will always be here
Watching over everyone
I will be their own angel
Till the kingdom they come

Late night
Can't sleep
Thinking of all the things
Happening to me
Happening right now
And all I can think is why me, why now
What do I do how can I prepare
What will happen when I'm not there
But how can I know if people will even care
I've messed up so much lost so many friends
But soon it won't matter because soon I will end
It isn't long now I lost three weeks so far
Time flies so fast
Leaving me in the past
And when that does happen I hope it won't hurt
But if I does then let it be over quick
Let me pass in my sleep
Ending in a dream

Going on an adventure
With Alex, Levi and Claire
We're running down the pathway
Climbing up some stairs
This is so exciting
What wonder what's out there
Sneaking out to meet them wearing black so we don't get caught
We get to where we're going
And the stars all shine so bright
Welcoming us out here with their shining twinkling light
Then Levi brings out the bottle
Shots every time someone laughs
Soon the ground is spinning
But I'm cozy and I'm warm
Lying in the grass
Staring at the stars
This is my home among my friends and now I don't feel so alone
My head is pounding
I feel like shit
Whispers turn to screams
I'm so done with it
Screeching, terrible pain
I feel like I'm dyeing
But it's not my time yet
Unless it's coming faster
But I'm not ready to go
It's probably just the hangover
Coming to say hello

Punishing me for last night
For sneaking out
But we didn't get caught
So it's all right
Now I just need to find a way
To get this monster
Out of my head
You sound so smug
Like you just figured out he would
Like you're the most important person ever
But your just one stupid girl
The world doesn't revolve
Around your feet
You stand there looking so innocent
But really you're about as nice
As salt is sweet
You tell us were incapable
You make us feel dumb
Yelling at us doesn't help anything
And you don't have to be so rude
When you tell us something is private
You probably shouldn't make an example of it in front of everyone
Because now we both know
Both me and Claire
Confided in you
And now we know
That's something that we
Can never ever do

Working so hard
I have one last school project and I want to get it done
I need to have something to show for all my hard work
So that when I'm gone I will have at least existed
Contributed to society
So that if someone looks up my name they will see what I've done
And be proud of me
They will read my words and feel my struggle
And they will understand what it feels like
Waiting for death
Knowing that no matter what you try you can't do anything to stop it
And they will be with me when it takes me away
Crying all the while
Throughout my last days
And so I have to get this done and over with
Have to write my story
So the world know about me
So that I'm not just one of those eighteen meaningless deaths per second
So that I make an impact
And don't just live and die
Unknown

Liz:

An Unexpected Turn is an incomplete 50,000 word young adult novel. Lana Gibbons is a young and naïve teen who must face the consequences of her dangerous choices in order to earn the trust of the man she admires.

An Unexpected Turn

The air was cold that night, especially for May. The midnight breeze sent shivers down my spine the minute it touched my skin. I don't remember exactly what happened in those few short hours, but I do remember chunks of it. It was the night that started it all, the night that would cause me to lose my mind in the end.

I sat on a couch at an unfamiliar party, filled with unfamiliar bodies and unfamiliar faces. The room was spinning from the amount of whiskey I had gulped down, and for a one hundred fifteen pound girl my body should have collapsed hours ago.

"Hey hun, how are you holding up?" A high-pitched voice asked.

I lifted my gaze to find Rain standing two inches from my face.

Rain. The petite brunette who first introduced me to this crazy crowd. The most manipulating yet amazing girl I had met in my time of living.

I held a thumb up, "Doing great."

She giggled, flashing a perfect set of pearly whites. I had only known her a week, and for that past week we had been doing nothing else but partying.

My mom had just been sent to rehab. Started off as drug dealing, ended up as drug addiction. I had to move from Nanaimo to Maple Ridge, where my dad was renting a small place until he could make enough money to actually buy one. He was a carpenter, but business was slow right now, so that meant money was, too.

I was never much of a drinker. Smoked a little pot, sure, but never liked what alcohol did to me. It turned me into someone I wasn't. Turned me into my mother.

Apparently the no drinking days were over though. Cigarettes, whiskey, Ecstacy, you name it. I was nothing more than a teenage mess, and I was okay with that.

"Hey babe," Rain shook my shoulder, shattering my thoughts, "I'm about on the same level as you and am in no condition to drive. I'm going to crash at Ryan's tonight. You know the cute cashier I met the other day? Anyway, my friend Beau is going to give you a ride home, he's the DD. Love you girl, prepare for tomorrow!" She kissed my cheek and left me with my head in my hands.

About five minutes had passed before I sensed someone else standing in front of me. I looked up to find a pair of ocean blue eyes, pouring into mine.

"Hey," a hand reached out to shake mine, "I'm Beau."

"Lana," I replied, letting my head drop towards my knees, "I'd shake your hand but I'm not sure I can even move right now."

I heard him chuckle, "You sure you're drunk? You don't sound too bad."

"Ability to speak is fine, ability to move...well that's a different story."

"I may be able to help you with that," I could hear the smile in his voice. Next thing I knew, my arm was draped over his shoulder and we were on our way out the door.

When we got into his vehicle, the spinning had cleared up enough for me to see his face. I turned to examine him and found myself in awe.

His hair was a sandy blonde, his jaw line out of this world, and his skin covered in the perfect tan. Whoever the hell this guy was, I needed to find out more about him.

"So..." I began before realizing I had nothing to say.

"So," he started the truck, "Beau Richards, graduated two years ago, been sober four. Rain gave me your address by the way. I'm the designated driver for these parties. The host, Paul, is my little brother. You?" He kept his eyes on the road.

That was fast. "Uh, Lana," I answered, "that's about all there is to know about me. Sober four years though? That's insane." And super lame.

"Not really, it's not bad. Sucks pushing drinks away, but it's better than ending up like the rest of my family." He lit a cigarette. Not a drinker, but a smoker. Hot.

"What's up with your family?"

His expression hardened. I stared at the floor as I felt his eyes travel over my skin. When I finally lifted my head, we were in my driveway.

"Let's save the question for another time," he whispered with his eyes still on me.

I nodded. I reached into my bag and pulled out a pen attached to a notepad. I wrote down my phone number and left it on his dash.

"Let me know when you're ready to answer some questions," I smirked, hopping out of the truck.

"Will do," he answered in amusement.

I thanked him for the ride and watched him back out onto the road. After I waved goodbye and headed inside, I already knew that I would be seeing him again.

Creative Writing class

Poetry

Hayley:

Ice cream in the evening,

in a golden,

autumn park.

The sun is on its descent,

casting its dying light across the

quiet town.

I observe from a distance.

I know I stand out

with my grayscale body

and snow white hair.

Yet, I go unnoticed.

I keep watching.

The young girl in the park sits alone.

She curves over the bench

like a broken vulture;

hunched, but too hurt

to hunt.

I can feel how lost she is, and I know

that it's time.

The sun is falling lower, tainting the scene with red

as I approach.

I know the place is
falling to pieces behind me now.
It's pulled into my back
and
devoured.
This memory,
the emotions and feelings
are torn to pieces
within my being.
It grows cold.
Her last memory is falling apart
at my hands.
I feel a surge of emotion before it melts
into my bones.
Now, her mind is gone.
I forage for memories, and fill my being with them.

Veronica:

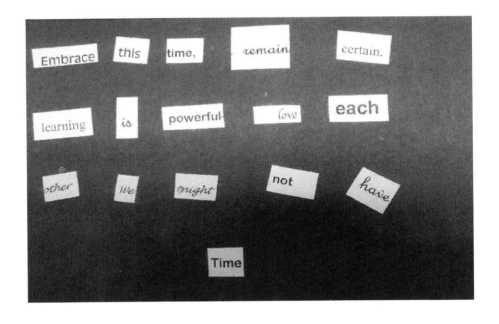

Kevin:

As I fly

Into the sky

I can barely feel my wings

heal

but when I fell

through the earth

it was the

first

time

I've felt hurt

as I fell through the earth

I could barely feel my wings singe

but when I flew into the sky

it was the first time

I felt alive

Celeste:

Hannah:

Devil

I can promise you

That there is a little bit

Of devil

In her angel

Eyes

You may not see it,

But I do

She made her promise

To you

That she would never hurt anyone…

But

She crossed her fingers

Behind her back

As she

Whispered to herself

You're

Not

Just

Anyone.

Will:

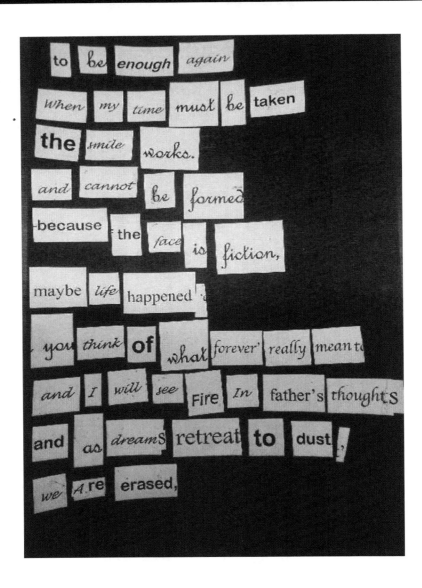

Jessie:

Songbird

He lived in The Rose,

but he was not beautiful.

He was shattered and

infected.

Addictive, like the thick wisps in his lungs.

Sweet, like sugar.

But we know that candy is never

good for us.

Bathed in gold, but he was no man of glamour.

For beneath layers of lace, satin and

French perfume,

there is a gentle boy, blanketed with shyness.

And me?

A bonfire.

Bright, dazzling,

dangerous.

I had issued a warning.

A flag waving high, emblazoned with words intending to repel.

But he was

fearless.

Unafraid of being charred.

He said; 'Oh, how I know that the wine plays tricks on your tongue.'

But I don't seem to notice when I numb these feelings with drugs.

A caffeine smile, and

a cocaine kiss.

Was all it took, and he was

captivated.

Flirting with the edge, he said;

'Paint me a heaven of love with your bloodied mouth.'

And after he'd gone,

I wished I had.

Jessie:

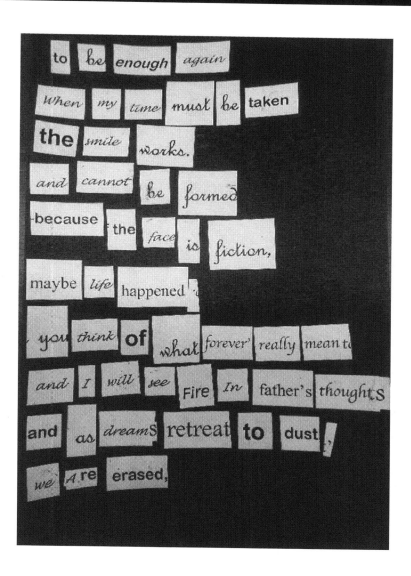

Armando:

Your Time Is Up

Tick,Tock Which do I choose?
Choices, Choices for the good?
Or Choices that could Break someone?
Or choices that could or destroy me.
It would be selfish if I chose what was best for me.
What about them? they have the same intentions as I do.
Tick, tock. My time is almost up.
I have dreams to pursue, but my future is already over.
They don't need me, I've live this world long enough.
To know that you won't escape sadness, you won't get a free pass
to happiness.
I can't kill innocent people no more.
He was the gun and I pulled the trigger.
Little Amy if you are reading this.
Don't make the same mistake as I did.
I was a fool to think I could save this world.
Looks like my time is up.
Tick tock.

Armando:

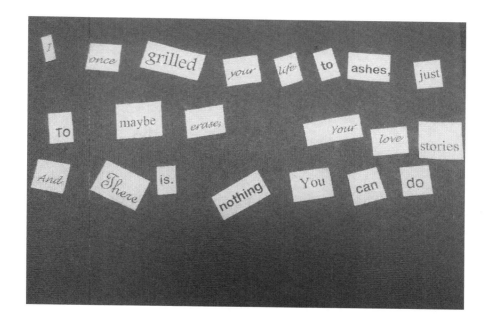

Liz:

The Same Shoes

6:03 a.m.

The time at which my eyelids wearily open

and my exhales turn soft,

The sky slowly changing from a dark charcoal to a smooth blue,

But the morning breeze still as

Cold

As it was at midnight.

This is why I am still here.

Still watching my chest rise

Then fall,

Still staring out the same window,

At the same time,

In the same room.

It is all so familiar,

The morning coffee soothing my goose bumps

And awakening my

Sore,

Tired mind.

The sheets a blessing to my icy skin but also a

Lonely

Reminder.

There is no change in this quiet routine,

No disruptions

Or new routes,

Leading me somewhere beyond this place with the same

Bland sky,

The same

Cold wind,

And the same

Lonesome mornings.

I am stuck on the same path that I travel every day,

Stuck in the same shoes

With the same

Boring

Laces,

Looking in the same direction that I have been

for the past two hundred twenty five days,

Searching for a different trail to take me back home,

Back to my

Colourful,

Creative mind,

Back

To

Myself.

6:03 a.m.

The time at which my eyelids wearily open
and my exhales turn soft,
The sky slowly changing from a dark charcoal
to a smooth blue,
And I am still here,
Stuck
In
The
Same
Shoes.

Core: Poetry

POETRY

JORDANN:

Warnings

My mother never told me
About the coldness
You feel when a boy mistreats you.
The coldness inside your chest
She never did warn me bout
Kissing boys whose mouths
Tasted like cigarettes and how
I'm slowly going to get addicted.
She never did warn me
But I wish she had
Because I'm slowly getting addicted
To the nicotine that lingered on his lips
Not once did she warn me about
Reality because I don't know
If I'm in it or not

JORDANN:

Isn't It Funny?

Isn't it funny

How we put our heart on the line

How we know we are going to get hurt

Yet we still fall anyway?

Isn't it funny

How we think someone is there to catch us

But they don't?

They say they will.

You trust them.

We are so caught up in the moment.

We are oblivious to what is happening.

We want it all.

The kisses.

The love.

All of it.

But then the person you thought you loves

Just walks away like you were nothing

But the were everything.

Isn't it funny?

NATASHA:

She Knows

She knows

But I was too blind to see

Even the worst storm's got to end

No one compares to you.

I think maybe I think too much.

You're lookin' so good in what's left of those blue jeans.

Dirty Diana

I will wait for you.

NATASHA:

FALLON:

I Miss

Don't you remember when days were simpler? Back on the playground with no worries in the world? Back when we weren't worried about exams, boys, makeup, or anything like that. All we had to worry about is who could make it to the swing set first. I miss those days when, when my mom would pack me a lunch and hug me before I went to school. I miss the days when I had to bring a walkie talkie with me to the park so my mom would be able to tell me to come home. The days where running around with your friends outside was normal. I miss the days back when you could act 100% like yourself without being scared or care about what people would think about you if they saw you in that pink tutu and fairy wings. I miss the days when people didn't judge us for who we hung out with, or who we talked to, what we thought was funny, or even just what we looked like. I miss the days back when people were honest but nice about it, when people genuinely cared about your feelings and wanted what was best for you. Grownups are constantly telling us that we're still kids and have lots of growing up to do, that might be true but for me right now, I'm as old as I've ever been and I miss being a kid...

FALLON:

The Smallest Things

The smallest things can change your life.
In the blink of an eye, or in a few milliseconds.
Something happens by chance
that sets your life on a course that you never planned,
even when you least expect it.
Takes you into a future you never imagined.
Where will it take you?
No one knows.
That's the journey of our lives.
Our search for the brightest light.
But sometimes finding the light,
means you must pass through
the deepest, hardest darkness.

NIAH:

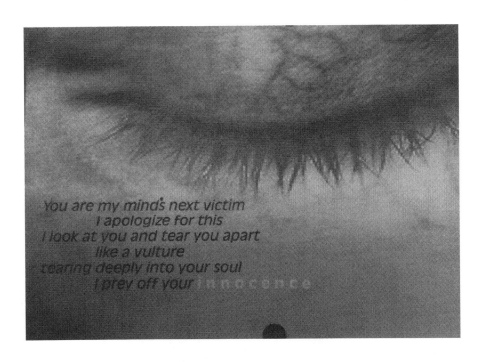

you are my mind's next victim
　　　　I apologize for this
I look at you and tear you apart
　　　　like a vulture
tearing deeply into your soul
　　　　I prey off your innocence

TIFFANY:

Books

Books are a doorway
to another universe.
Every book is like a new and different world.
The tales are never ending.
With pages swishing with imagination,
Reading is a motionless journey.

TIFFANY:

he

owes his

nightmares to

monsters,

who play with fire in

claws.

poor fool

lives

horrors in

heaven's

ash

LIZ:

We Are Women

May the women of the world be grateful;

For our small waists and thick thighs are admired,

Envied,

Our wide hips and delicate collarbones cherished,

Loved,

Every inch of us as breath-taking as the sunset,

Dazzling and

Divine.

May the women of the world recognize their strength;

Understand that our palms hold nothing but power-

We have as much force as a raging tsunami,

An active volcano preparing to erupt,

Take out towns with soul-shocking smiles and leave entire

cities breathless with just one

glance,

We are nowhere near weak or quiet,

We are magnificent,

Powerful,

We are strong.

May the women of the world learn to accept their flaws;

To smile at their freckled cheeks and giggle as they squeeze into their jeans,
We were not meant to be the same,
We were meant to shine like the midnight stars in July,
Not to hide because we cannot fit into a size zero,
Or because our teeth are nothing close to straight,
Since when did we start paying more attention to how we look rather than how we feel?
We are gentle like a morning breeze,
Yet harsh like a twisting tornado,
We are beautiful.
So let us be grateful!
Let us recognize our strength and accept our flaws!
Love ourselves as much as we love those who surround us,
And please,
For the love of god,
Let us take pride in the fact that
We
Are
Women.

Mrs. Bird Approved

Shawn Bird can be reached through
the contact page on her website:
www.shawnbird.com

Made in the USA
Charleston, SC
22 May 2016